Never Say

Never

Renee
you rocked this
cover.
I love it!   I love you!

Melinda Sutherland

Melinda Sutherland

This book is dedicated to those who have been affected by abuse.

To those who have loved and lost.
You will find happiness. Just never say never!

Prologue

I sob as I stand in the shower, letting the hot water bead down my body. I can't help but feel dirty. The sobbing is becoming uncontrollable as the images replay in my head. My legs give out and I slide down the steamed glass shower door. My ass collides into the cold white porcelain tub. As the water pounds down upon me, I sit unable to control my crying. After what seems like forever, I finally build enough strength to finish washing the filth off my body.

As I slowly start to stand on my still-weak legs, I grab the soap and washcloth; scrubbing my body until I rid myself of the filthy feeling. My body is now starting to shake from a chill that is running through me, turning my slowly pumping blood frigid in my veins.

What did I do wrong? Why did this happen? I thought he loved me... He was my boyfriend. He said he cared about me. Hell, he even said he loved me. Doesn't that mean he would never betray me? I thought we were happy. I was happy, happier than I've ever been. Why did he hurt me like   this?

So...About Me

My name is Amanda Nelson. I am a quiet but spunky girl from the North Shore of New England with beautiful light golden blonde hair, emerald green eyes, and a slender figure. I am fifteen years old.

My life thus far has been witness to many disappointments and mistrusts. But as I have watched my loved ones endure more than their share of pain, I keep my pain inside to prevent them from suffering any more than necessary.

To survive, I have had no choice but to grow up faster than most, often taking on responsibilities of an adult, though I am still young in my mind. I never felt that I had a real childhood. I saw things no one should have ever seen. At night I had to listen to the loud noises, the yelling, glass shattering. My mother's screaming and crying. Her life repeatedly shattered, her heart broken beyond repair.

I never wanted that life for myself. All I wanted was to be loved, to be understood. I wanted to find someone to understand me and love me. To comfort me. I thought maybe I had found that...until the day it was all stolen from me.

I can still remember my first meeting with Dr. Baker, whom my mother had insisted I go see because I never slept. I always had a hard time sleeping, and when I did, I was always awoken by nightmares. It was a beautiful day in late October. The sun was shining as the orange and yellow leaves were blowing around in the light breeze. It was the beginning of my freshman year at Roosevelt High. I wished I didn't have to go but my mom said it was time for me to open up and share my feelings, if not with her than with someone neutral.

My palms sweaty, shoulders slumped, I trudged up the steps to his office. Stalling, I tried to do a half turn but my mom grabbed my shoulders to promptly turn me back to the door. My heart was practically beating out of my chest as I tried to get air. Oh man I wanted to run. I really didn't want to share my thoughts or feelings with anyone, especially not a man I just met. I would have preferred to continue smiling through my life as if all was great. My stomach was flip flopping from nervous anticipation. Before entering I thought I would just stay quiet. That maybe if I didn't speak that all this would go away.

"Amanda Nelson, it's nice to meet you," he said. "I'm Dr. Baker."

I nodded, saying nothing. Instead of looking at him, I looked down and picked at my fingernails. My mother returned to the waiting room. After a few moments of uneasy silence alone with Dr. Baker, he tried to make small talk with me, to put me at ease he asked if I played sports, what my hobbies were, those kinds of things. Not wanting to be rude, I answered him, but kept it to simple, with one-word replies. When the questions became more personal, I stopped answering him. I wasn't use to opening up to people. I always kept a smile masked on my face, hiding my fears and pain inside.

"Amanda I know this is hard for you. I can tell by your simple answers and expressions that you do not want to be here. So let's try this. Your mother told me that you like to write. So between now and our next session, take some time and write your feelings and thoughts down. When you come in you can bring your notes to me. I will read what you wrote, and we can go from there." He paused, waiting for my response. When I nodded he reached over and grabbed a small book off the table, then handed it to me. I flipped through the pages. A new journal. "Dr. Baker, I do keep at journal already. I try to write in it daily."

"Amanda to make things a bit easier for us why don't you take that journal and write in it for our sessions. Maybe start off wherever you may feel the most comfortable with, I'd suggest maybe start with your childhood. I am only here to help and if you won't talk to me then try writing to me instead."

Upon completing the session, I met my mom in the waiting area and we walked out to the car. She didn't ask about what Dr. Baker and I talked about and I am glad she didn't. I wanted to reflect on a few things he said while they are fresh in my mind, so I was glad that we didn't really speak much in the car.

When we got home I went directly to my room. Getting comfortable on my bed, I just sat there and listened to music, and stared down at the blank pages in my new journal. I'd never had a problem writing in my journal before, but now I was at a lost for words. I doodled in the lines instead until the words came to me. After a few minutes it was all coming to me. I knew what to write and where to begin.

Dr. Baker-

As I sit here thinking about where to start writing and what to say exactly, I can't believe I am actually going to write this stuff down and let someone read it.

I am not comfortable sharing. It has always proved better for me to bury it inside. Talking about my feelings is not something I do well, since it is hard for me to trust and open up. Plus I never really felt that anyone would care or want to listen, as most people do have their own problems to deal with.

I guess I could start from the beginning. Paint a picture of my life so that you can have some understanding of how I got to be here to be a patient in your office in the first place.

I am always walking around with a smile plastered on my face, to hide the truth and pain. Since I was a very young girl anytime someone asks how I am doing, I automatically say, "I am fine, just great," and change the subject, especially if I am speaking with someone I could potentially break down and tell everything to. My mom loves me and is always trying to help me. I just feel as though I cannot tell her certain things.

My mom has helped me in a way she doesn't even realize. She's the one who always told me, "You know honey, you can write your feelings down and you don't need to let anyone see them. You can just write and then throw them away, keep them, or whatever you want." So I have done this every night, even if it is only a sentence or a word for the past few years.

So I guess I'll start at the beginning, to let you know why I am here.

My life has been a complete mess since the day I was conceived. What I mean is, I am happy to be alive but I had been through some deep shit for someone my age. I think it's time that I work on some of it. I need to get a clear head and make sense of it all so I can move on.

You suggested I start with my childhood so here it is as brief as possible.

My mom, Laura, was sixteen when she had my older sister, Samantha, and nineteen when she had me. She was divorced from Samantha's father shortly after having her, and started seeing my dad, Steve, when she was eighteen, though they had met when they were kids. They were good friends until they drifted apart around the time when my mom got pregnant with my sister and dropped out of school.

My dad has always struggled finding his place in life, same as my mom. As for my dad, he worked at the fish factory where he packed and shipped fish all over the world. He also had a few side jobs, anything he could find for a twenty-one-year-old without a college degree. My mom had a few different jobs here and there but never anything steady. When I was one, my dad was freaked out with the way his life was going and he bailed on us. Depressed and anxious, he felt as though he had to leave. In order to give his daughter the life he felt she deserved one day, he needed to better himself.

My mom tried to be civil and keep us in contact, but that became increasingly difficult after he accepted a job offer from a local fisherman. His new position took him away for long periods of time, and I rarely saw him while I was growing up. Once in a blue moon, I would go stay with him at his place. Although they were very short stays, I stole every moment I could to spend with my dad. He married his new wife, Sandy, when I was three. Then when I was almost five, my baby brother, Matthew, was born. Sadly, I didn't get to see him much either.

Life, it seemed, was perfect for them. I, however, was stuck living with my mom and all of her drunken, loser-ass, abusive boyfriends. The three qualities you always look for in a man, right?

A few of them beat the shit out of her when they came home drunk. Believe me; I witnessed more of that than any child should have. A few of them had the decency to at least stop when I came in the room, others didn't seem to care. The ones that didn't stop saw me, then turned and would keep at it, as they yelled and swore and screamed at me. They called me names and said terrible things to me, like "you fucking bastard," "little bitch," and "cunt," followed by something like "get the fuck out now before I come get you." There was constant fighting, yelling, and screaming when I was growing up. We moved a lot, probably about eight or nine times, by the time I was fourteen.

At that time, my sister was happy, living with her dad, stepmother, and stepsister. I saw her on weekends. Really only here and there, even though she lived close by. I, on the other hand, continued to live with a very unstable mother.

My mother was now into drugs and alcohol. At the ripe age of five, I remember getting myself dressed, making my own breakfast, and then walking the ten minutes alone to school. One good thing was that we got on welfare because my dad didn't pay us any money, so at least we had food on the table. I remember before welfare, my mom would wait until I ate before she did. She always pretended to clean and busy herself, but then I realized it was because there might not be enough food for the both of us. When I was seven, the truth came out about my dad and why I didn't really see much of him. He thought my mom was a cheating whore and that I wasn't his child. It really hurt like hell that he denied that I was his child.

My mom bought me my first journal after we had a talk about my dad. She wanted me to be able to release what I was feeling, but I was only seven so I mainly drew pictures and tried to write some words. I wrote after school and on the weekends, usually because I had no friends to play with.

When I was eight, my dad and his wife divorced, and she took my brother and moved to the West Coast. On my ninth birthday, everything kind of changed for me. I got the best gift. My mom and dad were fighting over child support and my paternity, and I got to spend what felt like the whole day at a hospital getting blood drawn, which was just to confirm what was so painfully obvious to everyone, but him--that I was his daughter.

Now I got to spend more time with him, which sparked a new found relationship between us, and also between my dad and mom, cause he now gave child support. He was helping her out more, and I began spending more and more quality time with him. The biggest and best thing that helped our new relationship was that he apologized for having put me through so much with all the paternity issues. He then vowed to show me love and make up for all our lost time. I had held a lot of resentment toward my dad for not having been there when I needed him the most. That apology really helped me learn to let a little of the past go and focus on us and our future relationship.

When I was ten I met my two best friends, Mark and Ann. Mark came from Michigan moved in a few houses from us with his parents. Finally I had someone to play with. He has been my best friend ever since. I've only told him a little about my life, when he asked, but he knew and learned enough to really know me.

Ann and I met at school and we instantly hit it off. Mark, Ann, and I were mostly all in the same classes. Ann lived with her mom and dad, Holly and David, in a cute little house in the nice part of town. Her parents were the best. I secretly wished I could have parents like them. I always wanted a normal family with stability. After a few years of being friends we started calling each other "sis or sister" everyone always asked if we were. After all, we did kind of look alike except she was a tad shorter than I and had smaller boobs. Her hair was a bit darker than mine and she wore glasses. Ann and I were pretty much the only blondes around. Everyone else being, Portuguese, or Italian, and having dark hair, the town we live is just so happens to be one of the oldest fishing ports. So it holds many of people that originally migrated here for the fishing industry alone.

My dad still worked for the same company, although he had been promoted to the vice president of sales by then, which helped us more financially. My mom attended NA meetings to get sober and was starting to act like a real mom, and the drunk boyfriends were gone.

By the age of twelve, my life became very busy. Mom was doing excellent and she had been sober for almost a year. She went to a lot of NA meetings while trying her hardest to stay focused and on track. She had found a new man, too. Jim. I really liked him; he was a good guy, finally. I knew after meeting him a few times and spending time with him, that he was different from the others. He was very kind and was super generous. Best of all, Jim didn't drink or use drugs. Not having any children of his own, Jim had taken to me treating me just like a daughter. We genuinely bonded and I looked up to him as a father figure. It was such a weird transition for me at that time, going from having no one in my life that I could rely on to all of a sudden having a mom and two men to help take care of me.

I don't know what Jim's job was exactly but I do know that he worked a lot of hours for the electric company. He was higher up in the chain because he was always dressed in a suit, he also mentioned something about being the boss once. Jim never hit my mom, and I think he really loved her. It really showed when they were together. I thought they would get married. He had spoken to me about it once when he took me out for ice cream, telling me how he wanted us to move into his house, but mom wanted to wait until she got her nursing degree, something she started working towards after rehab, but we ended up moving before she finished, right after I turned fifteen.

My life dramatically changed when we moved in with Jim across town. The move was a hard one for me. I was not going to be living a few houses from Mark anymore and it was also the start of my freshman year of high school.

Since I never really made friends before, except for Mark and Ann, it was so hard for me to fit in. Finally I met Kelly, who was really cool and kind of popular. Kelly lived with her drunken dad and an older brother Rob. While her mom was still alive somewhere, she just didn't know where. We all spent time together, Kelly, Mark, Ann and I. We did everything together from shopping, studying, and sleepovers.

My mom was busy finishing up with some of her nursing classes. She had continued going to NA meetings as well to stay on top of her addiction. That's about when I started sleeping out a lot, and hanging out at Kelly's more. Her house was where we would all hang out. Kelly started partying with her brother and his friends on the weekends. Their dad was away at his girlfriend's place in New Hampshire. So needless to say since we hung around that's when we started partying too. Except for Ann. She didn't party with us. Her parents were super strict and watched carefully over her life.

So I think that catches you up to speed on my life until now.

Early December

I just finished getting my makeup on when my mom walked into my room.

"Honey, are you about ready to go to see Dr. Baker? We have to leave within the next five minutes."

"I'm all set. Hey Mom, I don't really know where or when something in me changed but I'm actually looking forward to this session."

My mom turned her head slightly to the side, while almost squinting at me as if to try and see if I was telling the truth. She smiled. "Okay, well then grab that journal and let's go before we are late."

We drove in silence and Mom dropped me off in front of Dr. Baker's office. She wanted me to do this on my own. Before I got out of the car, I turned to her and said, "Mom, I don't think I've ever really told you, but I'm so very proud of you and the changes that you have made with your life."

She smiled wide, putting her hand on my arm and said, "Thank you Amanda I appreciate that. It really means a lot to hear you say that. I am also so very proud of you for taking this step. I know that your life has been hard, and for that I'm so very sorry. I'm sorry for all that my stupidity has put you through."

As I sat there listening to my mother say these words to me, I hadn't realized that I was crying until I tasted the salty tears on my lips. I was trying to stay so strong and not show my feelings. I turned to my mom lightly wiping the tears. I leaned over and gave her a great big hug and a kiss on the cheek.

I then pulled back, wiped my face again, and said, "I know that things have changed over the past couple of years, but please know that I believe in you. I love the strength and courage you have shown while pulling through to find yourself and your happiness. I really look up to you for that,

Mom." I gave her another kiss and told her I would see her soon.

"I have a few errands to run. I'll meet you in the waiting room when you're finished with your appointment."

As I got out of the car and walked to the building, I was clutching so hard onto my journal that my palms were all sweaty. I checked in with the secretary and she told me to go right in, that he was waiting for me.

While he read my journal, he had me fill out a questionnaire about insomnia. I was distracted and I couldn't help but wonder how this session would go. Would I ever be able to sleep at night and feel safe? He finished reading and then started right into our session with no hesitations. "Amanda how did you feel after writing about this? Can you put it into one word?"

I sat there for a moment thinking of the right word to use. Then all of a sudden I blurted out, "Hope."

"Hope?" he asked.

"Yes, hope," I replied. "I feel that after writing it all out, I really had to stop and think while taking a look at my life. I had to look at all the twists and turns my life has taken in the last few years. The positive changes that had been made after the negatives. It just gives me hope in that no matter how bad things got...it wouldn't stay that way. Hope gave me the strength to know that there was no reason to give up...as it would get better. It just might take a little extra time."

He seemed satisfied with my answer and we went on with our session, with him giving me some advice on what to think about and what aspects to reflect on. I left the appointment very comfortable with how it all went. He didn't judge me for anything. Feeling secure enough that I might be able to actually talk at the next session, rather than having him read what I wanted to say. I will keep writing in my journal as that will never stray from that, it has always been my one and only outlet in life.

***

But the following week, my life was forever changed. I met a guy at Kelly's house. We were sitting on the couch watching TV when Mark walked in with a few guys trailing behind him. Mark strolled over to us and Kelly jumped right up and gave Mark and the guys a hug. She clearly knew these other two guys. Mark plopped down next to me and kissed me on the cheek while putting his arm around my shoulder squeezing me gently. He then introduced me to the guys.

Kelly was hanging on one, who's name was Mikey. He smiled at me and said, "Hey."

The other guy was just standing there with a smirk on his face. I looked over to him and he nodded and said, "Hey, cutie! I'm Brad. Marks older, yet very sexy cousin. You must be Amanda," he said, and I smiled awkwardly, feeling my cheeks get hot while thinking to myself...holy hell Brad is super hot. "I've heard so much about you," he said.

I said "Hi," and started to turn and talk to Mark when he got up. He then leaned back down and said quietly in my ear. "Stay away from them, they are too old for you," he said while Kelly took the guys into the kitchen to get a drink.

Brad was so good looking. He had dark eyes and dark hair that was kind of flowing, not short. Just looking at his hair made you want to run your fingers through it. He was a bit tan for winter. Well, anyone was tanner than me anytime of the year. I was white as a ghost. Not to mention he smelled so good. That was the first thing I noticed about him. I don't know, maybe it was because Kelly's house smelled of stale cigarettes.

Never in a million years did I think he would ever even talk to me, but he did. I was sitting on the couch watching Van Wilder. He came into the room and sat in the chair next to the couch. We sat for a few minutes not saying much to each other. A very funny part then played on the movie and I started laughing so hard, I almost cried.

He then spoke and said that this was one of his favorite movies. I couldn't believe it cause it was my favorite movie too. He then got up and said he was going to the bathroom. At the same time Kelly, Mark, and Mikey came back into the living room, Mikey taking the chair that Brad was just sitting in. Mark sat to my right and Kelly sat on the floor in front of Mikey, between his feet.

When Brad came back into the laughter-filled room he smiled and casually took the seat to my left. We all watched the rest of the movie together. Just about at the end of the movie Kelly's brother came home with one of his friends, Greg. Everyone got up going into the other room with Rob and Greg. Everyone except for me and Brad that is. We sat and talked for a bit while a rerun of Friends played.

"So Amanda question and I want your honest answer, no saying what you think I want to hear either." He flashed a smile at me that gave me instant butterflies.

As I felt my face flush I wondered what the hell he was going to ask me. He seemed like a sweet guy. He did have a bit of a devilish look in his eye though. I smiled back at him and responded a little uneasy, "Yeah ok what?"

He chuckled lightly then asked, "So blonde...real or bottle?" Raising his eyebrow at me while he waited for my answer.

There was something about him that just seemed as though he was not your typical senior guy. I mean why the hell would he care if my hair was natural or not? Rolling my eyes at him but then putting my focus back on the TV, I didn't want to seem overly excited that he was showing interest. I was trying hard to just play it cool. I then blurted out, "Why does it matter?"

"Well I have always had a thing for blondes but they are a rarity around here ya know?"

Turning my head I took my focus away from the TV, resting my head on the back of the couch I looked into his eyes. I sat there just looking at him for a moment trying to figure him out. Is he for real right now?

He turned to me and said, "So? Do the drapes match the carpet or what?" All the sudden he burst into a loud laugh. He put his hand on my arm then said as he looked as though he was trying to stop laughing. "I'm just kidding with you but the look on your face was priceless. So are you a real blonde or not?"

Looking at him with wide eyes, in shock he just said that I finally answered his question with slight un-amusement "I am a true blonde, Brad. Just look at my eyebrows!"

After a few minutes of silence I got up to go to the bathroom I stopped by and talked to Kelly 'cause I saw that the bathroom was occupied. She was sitting at the kitchen table with the guys playing poker. I bent down and quietly but quietly asked her about Brad. "Hey, Kell, what's up with Brad. I don't really know to much about him."

Her response about him was one that I wasn't really hoping for but I listened to what she had to say. "Not much to say really. He's your typical fucking guy. He is cocky and kinda is a player. I think he sleeps around a lot."

Not really knowing what to say to all that I kept it simple. "Oh okay thanks for the info. I spotted one of the guys come out of the bathroom so I took my opportunity to leave the conversation.

I didn't sense that when we talked. He didn't have a cocky attitude anyway. As I walked into the bathroom I thought to myself that I would make my own decision about him. I wrote in my journal that night:

I met the hottest guy today. His name is Brad and I got this warm feeling and butterflies in my belly when we talked. He seems like a really great guy, except both Mark and Kelly warned me off him. I am going to give him a shot anyway and see how things   go.

Brad

We started hanging around together more in the weeks following. Kelly had started hooking up with Mikey. We all watched movies and went to the mall together.

Brad and I didn't really spend a whole lot of time alone together for the first several weeks, except when Kelly and Mikey disappeared for a little into the other room. We usually sat and watched TV and talked during that time. He never even really touched me. Only putting his arm around my shoulder or my back with his hand resting on my hip. But nevertheless, was always sweet and courteous. I didn't see any of the player everyone made him out to be.

But by January, the time we spent together definitely started to get much more advanced than I was comfortable with. At first it was okay. Our alone time consisted of just making out, just kissing, no real touching. After a while it moved to a hand up the shirt. I was okay with his hands gripping and groping my large breasts. I was a C cup, which is pretty big for a fifteen-year-old. It was uncomfortable at first but then as the weeks went on it didn't seem uncomfortable to be with him like that.

The touching lead to us making out more and he would grope my breast, and make some sly move, holding my hand and bringing it to his upper thigh and over his bulge. He started to get more bold as time went on. I only touched him over his jeans though. I wasn't ready for more than that.

I had my next visit with Dr. Baker. We had a really good session. We talked about the metal and physical abuse that my mother and I went through. I told him that my mother and I talked a little about those times and were trying to communicate our feelings about it all. I did bring up Brad, I told him that I was excited to have found a new friend. That Brad and I were getting to know each other. I talked about the fact that I got butterflies when we talked or when I knew I was going to be seeing him.

By the end of February, we started spending less and less time with Kelly and Mikey, and Mark wasn't hanging around with us as much either. He was starting to fail some classes and his parents were keeping him home to study and catch up. Mark kept telling me not to get to close to Brad, but I brushed his words off.

One night we were all hanging out at Kelly's we were sitting on her couch and Kelly and Mikey were in the kitchen playing cards. Brad and I were making out on the couch. The next thing I know I hear the front door open. We broke off our kiss and I spotted Mark. He looked pissed off. Mark grabbed Brad by the arm and said, "Hey come with me for a minute!" Brad looked back at me, shrugging his shoulders as he stubbled out of the room as Mark pulled him along.

I could hear Mark yelling at Brad. It sounded like they were on the other side of the apartment but I could hear muffled yelling. I started to get up to go try and listen in on what all that yelling was about, when Kelly walked into the room. "Geesh what the hell is wrong with them two?"

I started to respond to her when Mark stormed back into the living room. He gave me a fake smile as he approached me and said, "Hi." When he got to me he gave me a kiss on the forehead and said, "Please remember what we talked about. I have to go I just came to grab my jacket I left here last night."

I pulled back from him. I went to ask what he was referring to when Brad walked back into the living room. Mark turned to look at him then turned back to me whispering "Amanda just remember what I said. I will talk to you later." He kissed my head again and then left. Naturally I then turned my attention back to Brad.

"Brad! What the hell was that all about?"

I stood there while resting one of my hands on my hip. I have no clue as to what just happened but from the tension that was in the room with them two, along with his quietness, I was sure it had something to do with me. Now all I needed to do is figure out is why Mark got so mad at Brad and me for wanting to get to know each other. Why does he not want me with him? Looking at Brad I said, "Well are you going to stand there and stare at me or talk?"

He started walking toward me as Kelly got up from the chair she plopped herself into moments before and said, "Well I guess that's my cue to leave. I'm gonna go find Mikey." I nodded to her in agreement.

"Amanda, hey, sit with me. Let's talk." He touched my elbow ever so lightly directing me back to the couch. "You know how Mark can be sometimes with you. He gets so protective of you. Please don't tell him I said this but I think he likes you more than a friend."

I sat there with a look on my face that showed him that what he just said was totally ridiculous. Never in a million years would I believe that Mark would like me more than a friend. He is more like a brother to me, he's one of my best friends. "Brad no way, you're crazy for even saying that. Never mind even thinking it."

"What Amanda, are you kidding? Really? See how he just got when he walked in here to find us making out?"

"Yeah but what's the real reason behind him being so protective of me when it comes to you...keeping me away from you Brad? Why? What is making him want to protect me from you?" I sat there and stared at him waiting for a reply.

"Obviously it's cause I have slept with some girls. He's told me that he's afraid that I will try and sleep with you. I already told him that I'm not looking for that with you. I meant it to and I will tell you that myself. Amanda I am not looking to sleep with you!"

I sat there listening to him speak while I watched his eyes and the reaction he was making to my facial expressions. I just want to continue to give him a shot. His past of sleeping around is not what I should use to judge who he is. It's the way that he's treating me, the conversations we are having. The fact that he hasn't yet even tried to touch me.

"Brad I understand where the both are you are coming from. I understand his side. I myself am thinking you may think that I am like all the rest of the girls out there. Honestly that is not me. I am to young. I am not gonna have sex with you just cause you flash that smile of yours at me. I am not ready for all that yet!"

The look of shock on his face just told me that he wasn't expecting that from me. "What? Amanda I just told you. I honestly am not looking for that with you."

"Well Brad you should make sure cause it's not gonna happen. Really it's not!"

He leaned forward and kissed me on the cheek. "Really I am being completely honest with you here."

I was looking down tracing patterns on my jeans. As he placed his hand lightly on my chin lifting my face to his. "Amanda do you believe me? I only want to get to know you and nothing more unless you were truly ready for that."

I then couldn't help the small smile that creeped it's way to my face. He smiled back and then kissed my lips so tenderly.

After a couple weeks Kelly and Mikey were starting to be alone in her room for longer periods of time. Now Brad and I were no longer making out sitting or standing, we were now lying down on the couch, which got much heavier. One night we were at his house for a change and he said to me, "Amanda can we try something?"

I said, "No Brad. I'm not having sex. I've told you before...I'm not ready."

He replied with a sweet and calm, "No Amanda, sweetheart. Not sex. Here, let me show you. It's called dry humping we do it with our clothes on." It felt weird, but I kind of liked it. Of course, it was strange to me because I never had been touched like that. But it was okay because I would not let him get under my clothing.

That changed when he put his hand down my pants and touched me down there. While he was touching me, he grabbed my hand and put it down his shorts. It felt so strange to me; I never really explored my own body or touched myself. I didn't know what else to do, so I let him touch me for a few minutes. Then I stopped it when he slipped his finger inside of me. "Oh no!" I said rushed and scared, "Wait I'm uncomfortable with this Brad. I'd like for you to take me home please, now!"

As I stood quickly putting my shoes back on, he sat there on his bed, quietly watching me. He seemed kind of shocked that I stopped him but he remained quiet.

I couldn't tell if he was angry and masking the anger or being sincere as he apologized a few times during the drive to my house. I sensed some sincerity but in my head…I was freaked out by all this. I needed some time.

I ignored his calls for a few days. After listening to his messages I decided to just talk to him, so I called him and asked him to come over.

My mom was in the kitchen cleaning up after dinner. We sat in the living room and I told him I couldn't see him anymore. I was being honest with him, letting him know that I was no way near ready to go to those intimate places with him.

He replied, very quietly. "I'm so sorry, you just turn me on so much, something happens to me when I'm with you." He grabbed my hand, rubbing his thumb along my fingers, and continued speaking. "From now on, you'll be in control." He placed his hand on my cheek. "You can lead the way of how far we'll go. I just want to be with you, please give me another chance." He was very sweet about this whole situation, so I decided I could give him another chance. But if things get to be too much for me again I'd really need to back off.

The next few times we saw each other, he said romantic things to me like, "I love spending time with you alone, just holding you. I'll wait till you are ready to have sex, I really care about you" and "Amanda, you make me feel like I can be a better person. You just simply amaze me with your pureness and beauty."

March went by quickly. We had a lot of huge blizzards that completely buried us in our homes for days on end. During those snow days, I only talked on the phone with my friends and Brad, but we did manage however to talk pretty much every day. The times we did get to spend together were few. He again did remain a gentleman. He was beginning to pull me in deeper to him emotionally. There was no doubt about it that I was falling hard for him.

***

As I sat and talked to Dr. Baker I couldn't help but to feel excited about my relationship with Brad. "I feel that I am finally starting to feel happy for once. I love the way that I feel when I am with him. He always says things that makes me feel special. He is always telling me now much he loves my green eyes and how beautiful my hair is." As I spoke to him I wondered if he was sitting there silently judging me. So I made sure that Dr. Baker knew I wasn't crossing any lines I wasn't comfortable with. "Brad has kept things between us simple all we've done is kiss. I have made it a point to make sure that he knows where my comfort level is."

I left Dr. Baker's office and had a couple missed calls from Brad. I listened to his message. He wanted to take me to the movies. I called him back and told him to pick me up at my house in an hour. We ended up watching a comedy and laughed the whole time. He was a perfect gentleman the entire time. As for our relationship it was growing a bit stronger because he was respecting my wishes. As the weather got better, we began seeing each other almost every day.

I hung around with Ann and Mark one Saturday afternoon. We went to the mall did a little shopping, had lunch, and watched a movie. We ate lunch at the food court. We all caught up on what was happening in our lives.

I asked Mark, "Hey how are those grades coming along?"

"Well, they are coming up slowly. I am getting them back up enough to keep on the team so good enough for me. I am also off restriction that's why I am with you guys today."

Ann spoke up. "Mark I can help you get them up more. I have the time to help you."

Oh I couldn't resist getting on her case. "Yeah because all you do is study and go to school. You never hang out with us anymore. What about dating? Do you plan on dating anytime soon?"

Mark chirped in. "Leave her alone there is nothing wrong with being single."

"Amanda, there is nothing wrong with being focused on school. Besides I haven't found anyone I really would even want to date anyway."

"So what's going on with you and Brad. Is he pushing you yet? Ya know I warned him if he hurts you I will beat the shit out of him"

"Yeah Mark I got that. There is no need to fight though. He is being good. We only kiss and make out. Believe me that's nothing that I am uncomfortable with."

Ann spoke up "Well Sis I think we are too young to be dating and spending time alone but as long as he doesn't cross that line and try to push you to have sex, I'm cool with you dating."

THE NIGHTMARE OF APRIL

Then one day, things changed between me and Brad. It was a Saturday late morning in mid-April. It was a nice New England day. It was a little cloudy but the sun was shining and a nice light breeze blew through the crisp clean air. I heard a knock on the front door. We weren't expecting company today. I walked over opening it to find a nice surprise. Brad was standing there all cute and smiling with a fresh new haircut.

I smiled at him as he held up a white paper bag with the label of my favorite bakery. "Hey I stopped and got you a muffin. Sorry I didn't call I just figured I would surprise you."

A surprise it was for sure. "Brad that is so sweet of you. You know you can stop by anytime hey come in."

As I ate some of my muffin Brad was talking about how nice it was out today. "Amanda we should take advantage of this day and go for a walk. Maybe to the park or something."

When we left the house it started to look a little dark out to the east of the ocean. "Hey Brad I think a storm is gonna grace us today, maybe it's not such a beautiful day after all."

"Well we can try to make the most of it."

We strolled down the street hand in hand. He stopped us along the way and picked this beautiful wild flower and put it in my hair. "You are so beautiful and I love making you smile."

When we got to the park we swung on a swing for a little while as we talked about a few random different things. When it started to sprinkle a little so we decided to go back to my house. When we got inside we found a note from my mom, saying she'd gone grocery shopping. Jim was at work, so that meant we were alone. He has been over my house a couple times but not alone yet so I got a bit nervous. "Brad, do you want a drink or something to eat?"

"No I think I'm good. Let's go in your room and talk, listen to music, and play cards or something."

Brad went into my bedroom I followed a little behind him. He took a seat on my bed as he looked around my room. I wondered what he thought as he was checking out all my stuff. I lightly shutting the door behind me and he looked over to me and we made eye contact.

"Amanda?" he said, and waited for my response.

I raised a brow and half-smiled in curiosity as to what he was about to say. "Yeah?"

"I don't think I can see you anymore," he said.

Shocked, I looked at him with a puzzled expression and then kinda freaked out. "Why Brad, because I won't sleep with you?"

He furrowed his brow. "No, Amanda, it's not that!"

I put my hand on my hip and questioned him more. "Okay then what is it? You met another girl who will?"

He looked down at his feet. "No, I really like you, I would never hurt you like that." Pausing he then looked at me as he started lightly shaking his head. "Why do you think I have been so patient with you?" he asked. "It's because my dad is accepting a new job and we have to move. We are going next saturday to go sign for the house we are getting."

I looked at him with mass confusion, nearly shouting while throwing my hands the air. "Why am I just hearing about this now?"

He started to stand as he must have finally caught on to my extreme anger. I held up my hand as to tell him to stop. He stopped in his tracks and blurted out with frustration, "I didn't want to say anything until my parents said it was for sure."

Just as frustrated I spit out, "So you're just thinking about yourself? What about me? Don't you think you should have at least brought it up to me, maybe give me a heads up? I told you that I was starting to have feelings for you. But instead you come here and just drop this on me like I would be ok...like it wouldn't affect me?

He then again started to step forward as I halted him yet again. "Amanda, you are everything to me. You must know that. I care about you so much, and I don't want to hurt you!"

The look in his eyes now seemed so genuine. All of a sudden I had this strong urge to kiss him. I closed the remaining distance between us and put my lips to his. I don't know exactly why I had such a strong urge. Maybe it was the way he looked, sad, sincere, yet scared. He pressed his hand to the small of my back and started kissing me harder.

One thing led to another and we were making out so heavily my lips were starting to ache. We were rubbing our hands all over each other and now lying down on my bed. Then, I heard the front door open, it was my mom and she yelled out, "Amanda I'm home, are you here?"

"Ah, yes mom, Brad and I are in my room." I then quickly jumped off my bed and I turned the radio on low and grabbed a deck of cards. We sat on my floor pretending to have been playing cards.

She walked in, shaking her head. "Hey guys you know the rules. Just make sure to leave the door open, and no hanky panky," then she left to go put the groceries away.

We just looked at each other and shared a conspiratorial smile. I got up and went to the kitchen to grab a drink. Stepping over the bags blocking the path to the kitchen, I saw my mom on the phone in her room, having what appeared to be a very intense conversation. I walked back into my room pushing the door so it was mostly closed. Brad was back on my bed lying down with his arm draped over his face. I went over and sat on the edge of my twin-sized bed. He continued lying there, not saying a word. I felt his tension. While all I stood there staring at him all I thought was he wants to break up with me, but maybe he really doesn't want to hurt me...What will I do if I lose him?

I bent down and tenderly kissed his lips. Then he reached over and placed his hand on my back, gently rubbing up and down. He kissed me back and I could feel something different about this kiss. I was startled by my mom's voice as she was walking back to my room.

"Amanda!" She called as she got to my door. I sitting straight up and turning slightly as she entered. "I have to go to Jim's work. He forgot to bring something to eat." She stood there with a look of frustration on her face.

"Hey, Ms. Nelson. I'm leaving soon anyway." I felt his hand rest down on my arm. My mom shook her head as to say alright.

"Okay, Mom, maybe bring him one of the brownies we made last night. He loves those." I know that she doesn't like when we are alone. Maybe that's why she seemed aggravated.

She looked at me sternly. "I will be right back. I'm only driving across town and then straight back." She then left the room.

I lied down next to him and cuddled into his arm while resting my head on his chest. "Brad, are you going to break up with me now?" I blurted out.

Rubbing my back lightly he then lifted his head and looked into my eyes. "Amanda, no, I am not. I want to be with you even if there is no sex. I am fine with that." He then gently kissed the top of my head.

"Okay, Amanda I am leaving now I will be back in a half hour." My mom shouted as I heard the front door open.

"Okay, mom!" The sound of the front door closing was hard. I wondered why my mom was so upset. I think she would have asked Brad to leave if she was that uncomfortable. I started to get a little nervous as we were alone again.

We started kissing again. He was holding me tightly and the next thing I knew we were caressing each other again. Then his hand slipped into my pants. While he was touching me, he said, "Amanda, you are so wet!" Kissing me again quickly, he then pulled back slightly and stated, "I can tell you want me too!"

I didn't know what I wanted, but this felt good. He pulled the blankets up over us, grabbed the remote, and turned on the TV, I think to make my mom think we were just innocently watching a movie if she came back.

Brad pulled down my yoga pants down with his foot, resting them at my knees. I don't know why I didn't just get up right then, but I let him keep going. I was scared but I did feel safe with him. He hadn't done anything so far that was hurting or uncomfortable.

As he started fingering me, he began to move his finger a little more rapidly. Then he added a second finger and he said, "You're so tight and wet, I love it! I love you, Amanda." I froze. Oh my god he just told me he loved me. Not many people have told me that. I like how it sounded. I was kind of in a daze, shocked by his confession. He looked at me raising an eyebrow, as if waiting for a response.

"I love you too Brad!"

He kissed me with more force this time. He put my hand in his pants to touch his hardness. I was still in a fog. I had so many things running through my head, and all I was stuck on was the fact that he just told me he loves me.

Then he was on top of me trying to push his hardness inside of me. I didn't know how to feel about all this. He just told me he loved me, he told me that he would never hurt me. Was this okay? Could I do this? Oh my god, was I going to have sex?

No, no, no I am not. My brain is thinking and my mouth isn't speaking. I'm not there yet. I am not ready to do this, not now. I was not ready...

As I am watching him above me, my voice is not working. I am frozen. I am now feeling like I'm not even a part of my body now. He takes his hand to his mouth and spits on it. He then brings it back down, wiping it on my opening. That touch, him putting his hand on me...It unlocked me. "No" I whispered but barely audible. I felt a single tear slip down my cheek. "No." A second later, I hear this weird sound, it sounded kind of like a pop. I feel a burning, a pain. He just pushed it inside me.

"NO!" I say again, louder now, and loud enough that he should be able to hear me as I press my hands hard against his arms.

While this is happening he is not speaking much. He just says, "Oh baby, your so tight."

I am now hitting his arm harder, "STOP!" I am trying to move my legs but he is heavy on top of me and my legs are locked by my pants around my knees."This hurts, Brad! Please! No, no, no, I don't want to do this Brad. Stop!"

My tears are now flowing uncontrollably and I am shaking. I say it again, this time while I am hitting his forearm with all I have, trying to get him to stop."It hurts, Brad. Please stop!"

He then grunts and says "Oh yeah" between his teeth.

"Stop!" I cry, and I feel completely helpless as I cannot make him stop. "Noooo!" I scream as I cry out loud...

Then all the sudden he stopped. "Oh come on it's not that bad," he said. "But don't worry, I'm done now!" As he threw off the blankets, he lifted his weight off me and got up. He didn't even look at me while he pulled on his pants, as I laid there a hysterical mess.

I laid there in my bed crying as he slipped off to the bathroom. I heard the bathroom door open, then close. I heard the front door open. "I'm back."

Then I heard the bathroom door open again a second later, but he didn't come back into my room.

I heard him talking now to my mom. "Amanda and I were watching a movie, but she fell asleep."

I knew he told her that so she wouldn't come into my room and see me this way. I felt awful and I hurt. I was so sore. What do I do now? Then I realized he didn't even wear a condom! I didn't want this. Why didn't he stop?

He walked back in to my room. I laid there just staring at him, tears streaming down my face as I cried silently. He handed me a bottle of water, and said quietly, "Amanda I am sorry if that hurt, but next time it won't be so bad." I wiped my face off with my sheet and tried to speak, but he cut me off. "I'm going to go meet up with the guys, we are supposed to go to the Y to play basketball." He then leaned down and quickly, but barely kissed my forehead "I'll call you later!"

My mind was racing. I couldn't help but think and be completely confused. He left, he left me like this? Fucking bastard! He told me he loved me and didn't listen when I said to stop. Why didn't he stop?

I lay there, yet again, all alone, weeping but not able to move or do anything. All I could do was, think and cry. As I put my hand down to touch myself all I could feel was wetness, and that I was slightly swollen. I felt slimy, sticky, and in pain, and I lay there for a long time, growing more and more numb.

Eventually my mom came into my room and asked if I wanted dinner. "Not now I just woke up," I said. "I think maybe after I shower."

"Well I need to go do a few errands, and then I have to pick Jim up at work after. His car is still in the shop. We can eat when I get back then. I'm making soup tonight."

I finally got up several minutes after my mom left. I looked down at my bed; there was blood on my sheets. I was instantly scared and freaked out.

Emotionless, I ripped the sheets off my bed, put on new ones on, and brought the dirty ones to the trash. I needed to go take a shower, I felt so used, disgusting, and dirty! I wanted to get the feeling of Brad off of me.

I scrubbed the shit out of my body but I still didn't feel clean. So I turned the water up, as hot as it could go. I was probably now burning my skin, but I just wanted to feel clean again. I stood there for a few more minutes, finally turning off the water when it was starting to get cold again. I stepped out and dried off my body. Then I heard a loud knock at the front door. I threw on my fuzzy pink bathrobe, and headed out to the door. On my way there, I couldn't help think to myself, oh no what if it's Brad. Maybe he came back. I definitely could not see him right now. Not after what he...

When I got out of the bathroom, there was another knock at the door. I froze, and then came another knock. "Who's there?" I asked, hesitantly.

"Amanda it's me." Mark. "Please open the door. Come on its pouring out here." Relief washed over me as opened the door, not making any eye contact with him. He stepped in and practically shook off like a wet dog.

"Hey," I said, and at the same time he said, "Hey, I.." And then abruptly stopped talking.

I noticed I was playing with the belt on my robe. I wanted to just pull it tighter.

He must have sensed something was off. "Amanda, what's wrong?" he asked, and I stood there silent. A good minute passed before he said again, "Amanda! What's the matter, what's wrong?" He spoke loudly and reached out for my hand. I continued to stand there not saying a word or even look at him.

I couldn't tell him what had happened with Brad. "Amanda?" he said again.

Do I tell him? I thought I had to quickly just say something. "Umm, I, I think I'm sick," I said. "I'm getting the flu." He then reached down and put his hand to my chin, gently lifting my face up to look at his.

"Your eyes are bloodshot and puffy, not to mention you're all red," he said.

I quickly responded, "I was in the bathroom throwing up, and then I took a long hot shower."

He moved behind me, placed his hands on my shoulders, and gently pushed me towards my bedroom. "If you're sick, you should lie down, and get some rest." I then took a deep breath and hesitantly sat on my bed. Not wanting to ever touch this fucking bed again, actually, I'd love nothing more than to set this shit on fire. Mark left the room, and said, "I will be right back, and lay down will you." I got up turned the radio on and went back to lie down, cringing as I did.

When he returned several minutes later he had toast and a glass of ginger ale. "You need to eat a little if you have been throwing up," he said. "You don't want to get weak."

"Thank you, just put it on my nightstand, please. I'll nibble on it." I was lying on my bed with my eyes closed, trying to hide and feeling extremely anxious. I didn't want Mark asking me questions. If I slipped up and said something, it would be to him. I'd trust him with my life. For the past five years he'd been the one constant in my life. Out of all my friends and family, he was the one I spent most of my time with. Hell who was I kidding, if I was not alone, with Brad, Kelly or Ann, I was with Mark.

He sat down on the floor next to my bed, reached up, and stroked my hair. A few minutes went by and he stopped, he took his finger and wiped away a stray tear that had fallen down my cheek. I didn't even realize that I was crying. He said, "Hey what's wrong? You really don't feel well, do you?"

I hesitantly said, "No."

He was such a great friend, he rubbed my back to comfort me, while he was doing that, I heard the front door open and I twitched at the sound of the door closing. It was my mom and she was yelling to me that she was home. She then walked into my room and stopped at the sight she had just walked into.

Mark looked up to her and said, "Hey, Lauren, our girl isn't feeling very well."

My mom walked over touched my forehead. "Amanda, what's wrong, honey? You seemed fine this morning. You seemed okay up until you woke up earlier, after falling asleep while watching that movie with Brad."

Abruptly, Mark's hand stopped rubbing my back. "Brad was here today? You didn't tell me that. Did he know you were sick? He left you? What if something happened to you?"

Defensively, I said, "Mark I am fine just have the flu I think, I'm not dying!"

My mom spoke up and said, "I will go make a pot of soup." Then she left, closing the door. My mom knew that Mark and I were best friends and that there would be no hanky panky going on with us.

Mark's eyes pretty much burned a hole right through me. I could feel his intense stare. He finally spoke. "Amanda, you're not sick are you? Brad was here today did something happen, between you two? Did he break up with you?"

All I could manage was "No," while shaking my head. Then all of the sudden I started crying again. I feel so weak, why can't I stop crying? I thought to myself.

Mark spoke up with a tone to his voice I did not recognize. "What happened? Something happened. I can tell you are not alright. I knew it since the moment I saw your eyes when I got here. They were that bright green they get only when you cry."

I continued to be silent but cry. As the tears streamed down my face, his hand was wiping them away. He leaned over to where my hand was resting on the edge of the bed next to his head, and he ever so gently touched his lips to my hand, and kissed it. Then he was saying into my hand quietly. "Amanda, talk to me. Tell me what happened today? I know something happened. You're a mess. I am here and I am safe to talk to, you know that."

He took his face from my hand, and then placed his hand on my hair. "Whatever you say to me, it will stay between us. You know you can trust me, to take care of you. Come on now! Who gave you a piggyback, all the way home from school that time you tripped and fell, and sprained your ankle? Who took care of you, and stayed with you the first time you drank? Who held your hair for you while you threw up? Me, that's who, while Brad was off doing who knows what, with god knows who!"

I took a deep breath, trying to stop myself from crying anymore. I knew I should tell him what happened. He was right. I could trust him, and he would take care of me.

I can remember everything I felt at that moment, like it was yesterday. I remember...

I am scared because if I tell him, I am afraid he may say something to Brad. I'm terrified that everyone will find out, look at me different and I will hear soft whispers that I am a slut for having sex at age fifteen.

I am confused, and I don't know what to do. I wouldn't want anyone else finding out about this. Would he believe me when I tell him that I said no, and that I didn't want to? He knows that Brad was pressuring me into having sex, and that I didn't want to because I am not ready... Was not ready. Was, being the operative word, now that I am no longer a virgin. Oh my god, I'm not a virgin anymore.

I didn't want that to happen. And that's when it all finally clicked. I was raped! I said no, I said no, many times, I told him to stop, and I said no that it hurt. Damn it, I didn't want it. I took a deep breath, and another one. The tears streaming down my face, soaking my pillow.

I kept taking deep breaths, while trying to collect my thoughts on where to begin. Mark sat quietly on my bed, rubbing my back. I was finally starting to relax.

"I'm sorry Amanda, but I need to go to the bathroom, and I have to call my mom." I just gave him a grunt, not wanting to speak yet. I was more relaxed now, I could have fallen asleep, but I could hear my mom and Mark talking in the living room. I couldn't quite make out what they were saying as I lie there feeling completely alone, but now I felt more relaxed, knowing Mark was there for me. For the first time since this morning...I was   blank.

The Aftermath

I sat in my room, listening to Adele on the radio. Man, I love her music. Her voice is amazing, and the lyrics to some of her songs really inspire me. But listening to the song that was playing at this moment, "Melt my Heart to Stone," it was a dead-on description of my relationship with Brad. Yeah he definitely built me up and left me dead after he tore his way through me. Oh I was getting really angry I just wanted to punch something. I hit my fist hard on the bed. Ughhhh!

Powerful words, so fitting to the situation, to how I felt. Shit! Now I felt like crying again. But then Mark walked in, all smiles, carrying a bed tray with a bowl of soup and some crackers. "Something for you to eat."

As I sat up, I couldn't help but watch him, smiling and walking slowly, trying not to spill the tray. I thought to myself, I trust him, and I love that he does take care of me.

"Thank you! I am kind of hungry now. I only had a half of muffin this morning. I'm sorry I never ate the toast you made me."

He smiled back. "Shit, I barely ever want to eat anything I make either so it's okay. Well you really need to eat this up then. I was going to mention that, you are way too skinny these days." He sat down next to me as I ate.

"Don't make me eat alone. Go get a bowl."

He replied laughing, "I ate some already as I was talking to your mom. Sorry!" As he smiled and shrugged his shoulders.

I enjoyed a few more bites of my soup. "No worries, I can eat alone, I'm used to it." Blowing on another spoonful, I ate another bite.

My mom walked in my room and asked, "How's the soup Amanda? I would ask Mark but I already know that he likes it. He ate three bowls."

I gave him a shocked look. "You're a pig! Three?" I smiled in disbelief that he managed to eat that much in a short time.

He smirked. "Mmm, yes I had three bowls. But don't worry. I didn't eat it all," he said with a wink and a smile.

"Well Amanda it's getting late and I gotta go to bed. I have to work an early shift at the hospital in the morning. Jim is already asleep cause he had a headache so to keep the music down please?She came over and kissed mine, then Mark's forehead, and said, "Amanda my love, Mark, my pain in the ass, good night. Oh and Mark come with me, I will go grab you a pair of Jim's shorts for you to wear to bed." I almost spit out my soup.

I couldn't believe my mom was letting Mark sleep over tonight. He had slept over a few times before when we were younger. He also slept over once last winter because we had a really bad snowstorm, then again because she and Jim went away overnight to visit his family and they didn't want me to be alone. So I guess it's not that odd but still, we are getting older now.

Mark strolled back into my room holding a blanket under one arm, and a pillow under the other. I tried to hold back a laugh, seeing him in

Jim's oversized shorts but I couldn't help it. I laughed so loud, I almost burst into tears. Because, at that exact moment, LMFAO's "I'm Sexy and I know It," came on the radio. Absolutely priceless for this moment. When he realized why I was laughing so hard, he did a little strut.

He must have known that I needed to laugh, to just forget for a minute, because he kept at it. He was dancing around my room, gyrating his hips, and shaking his butt to the music. Absolutely by far the funniest thing, I've ever seen. We both were laughing so hard, I was crying.

I don't think I ever laughed so hard in my whole life. But then the song stopped and I couldn't stop crying; I suddenly realized that I was hurting and shouldn't be having that much fun. Mark came quickly to my side. He definitely knew that I was not okay, and he pulled me into the biggest and hardest hug I have ever gotten in my life.

"You know we need to talk, Amanda. You cannot keep whatever you're hiding in anymore. I know you're not sick. You haven't gone to throw up once since I've been here. Whatever happened today, we are going to talk about right now. I am here for you, I am here all night. I'm not going anywhere." His words made me feel like I could talk to him, and that I should. But, I needed a few minutes to get myself together.

I took some deep breaths trying to calm my nerves, while he just held me. I don't know how long we sat like that, but he never let me go. Finally I was ready to talk.

One more deep breath and I pulled back and gave him a look of extreme sadness. "Okay, Mark, let's talk."

He looked at me with sincerity and comfort in his eyes. "I am so relieved that you are going to talk to me. I was starting to really worry you would seal it all up in side." Squeezing my hand to let me know he was there and meant every word he said.

"Okay, but you are to not say anything until I am done talking. And you must promise me that you won't say a damn word to anyone. Not even Brad."

He gave me a puzzled look then held up his hand. "Pinky promise," he said. Still unsure of whether or not I was making the right decision,

I locked my pinky hard around his, took one last breath, and said, "Okay."

I started talking I told him all of what happened today while he just sat there listening intently.

"Anyway, there was something about the way he was acting, something different. I wasn't quite sure what it was. Even the way he was kissing me was different."

I started to become very nervous, and looked down to my legs as I continued. "I don't know what I was thinking because we were making out and fooling around, but it was nothing we hadn't done before really. Then I realized that he was trying to have sex with me."

I took a deep breath when I came to the realization again that he had said those words to me. "Mark he said it. He said he loved me." I sat there playing with my pants waiting for a response from Mark. I am not sure what I was waiting for him to say exactly. I sat silently and chocked back a few sobs.

He grabbed my hand. "He said he loved you?" he asked, looking at me with concern.

I gulped down the lump that was stuck in my throat. "Yes," I said, nervously. "It made me feel that I didn't want to lose him, didn't want him to leave me. I'm not sure if maybe that's why I said it back." I felt Mark's grip tighten slightly on my hand.

I was still not looking at him; I felt too ashamed. I couldn't believe that this was all happening. It still felt like a dream. Then I felt a wash of anger run through me, and I blurted, "I thought that he really loved me. Well, guess what? I'm a fucking idiot, because...Brad played me for a fool."

I was shaking my head in disbelief starting to feel like my blood was boiling. I shifted slightly as I started talking again. "Here I was thinking all this time he didn't want to hurt me. That he really cared about me. That he loved me" I now looked to Mark for answers because I certainly didn't have them. "What the hell, Mark!" I started crying uncontrollably.

He grabbed me and held me tight and whispered, "It's okay, Amanda. I'm here for you. But you need to tell me what happened."

While Mark held me, my head resting with my cheek on his shoulder. I couldn't help but to stare down at my bed, lost in a daze. I spotted a small smear of blood on my comforter, next to my knee. I stared down at the spot and realized I had more pain inside than I could have ever thought possible. I took a deep breath and felt as though I really needed this over. Today needed to be over. I pulled back from his embrace, looking down. I continued to relieve the nightmare.

"There he was above me. I knew what he wanted to do. I was frozen, completely terrified. I said no. Mark, I said no, but he did it anyway. He was inside me and it really hurt. I told him that it hurt, and to stop, I said no, that I didn't want to do it."

Mark gasped when he realized what I had just told him. I was still staring down but I could feel his gaze on me. He sat silently, lightly holding my hand. I think he was in shock from what I had just confessed to him. I didn't want to look at him. I didn't know if I could handle his eyes looking at me with disgust. I didn't know how to feel at this moment. I needed to say it, needed to say those words out loud to him. "Brad raped me." My hands instantly came up covering my face. I was now in hysterics.

Mark held me tight saying only, "I'm sorry!" He said it repeatedly as he held me while I cried. He lay down with me on my bed. Holding me tight for the rest of the night, not saying anything. He just let me cry and I finally cried myself to sleep.

I slept well that night, all things considered. I think that all that crying and stress, took more out of me than I thought. I was lying, facing the wall with an arm draped over my stomach. Then I remembered that Mark was with me, that he was there to talk and comfort me. He was truly my best friend, and I knew from that moment on, he would always be there for me.

I rolled over to face him and saw he was still sleeping. I kissed his cheek and slid out of bed. Oh man did I have to pee. I sat down on the toilet, and started peeing, oh my god it burned. My vagina was all sore.

I decided that a hot shower would help me feel better, so I turned the water on, took off my robe, and got in. I couldn't believe I was still in my robe, and that I had slept like that, naked under my robe with Mark in my bed. I was washing my hair when I heard a knock on the door and Mark ask "Hey can I come in? I got to pee so bad it hurts," Mark said.

"Yeah I know the feeling," I called back. "Come on in. But no peeking, okay?"

While he was peeing he said to me, "Hey, I'm gonna walk over to the store across the street I will be back. Do you need anything?"

As I was rinsing out my hair I said, "No I'm good, thank you. Hey Mark can you make sure you lock the front door behind you? I'll be done by the time you get back."

"Okay be back in a few"

I finished my shower, and went to my room to get dressed. I just threw on a pair of lounge pants and a t-shirt. I froze when there was a knock at the front door. I stood in the living room and stared at the door when I heard Mark say, "It's just me."

I opened the door and Mark was standing there with a little red heart shaped balloon and a teddy bear. He had a huge smile on his face. "Get well soon!" he said, and we spent the rest of the day together, and watching movies and making brownies.

Mark was reluctant to go, but it was his sister's birthday and he had to leave. "Amanda are you sure your okay. I can stay a bit longer or you can just come with me?"

Deep down I knew that I wasn't okay. I didn't want to be alone, but we both knew he had to go home and spend time with his sister and family. "Yeah Mark I am sure I will be okay. Just go I think I'm gonna go lay down for a bit or clean my room."

He then kissed my head "Well I am only a phone call away if you change your mind. Good night!"

"Fine I will call you if I need to but go, please go they are waiting for you. Tell her I said Happy Birthday!" He then left reluctantly.

I went into my room I turned on and up the radio. I needed a good distraction. I started rearranging things around my room. I needed everything around me to be different. I couldn't stand the site of my room anymore. I couldn't up and move my room but I could change its appearance. I moved all my mismatched furniture around to new spots.

My oak daybed to the wall my dresser was on, my white dresser that actually has five different colored drawers, I moved to the long open wall where my bed was. And my black desk and make shift vanity I moved to the far corner next to my closet.

I sat on my bed to take in the changes I made when I got frustrated and decided that I should write a bit. I opened my journal and wrote.

I am now left alone again. I tried to change my room but that isn't working. I still feel like I don't even want to be here. I am feeling so hurt, sad, and I am not sure how long I am going to feel like this. I don't know what to do. I am now laying here listening to the radio while I doodle at the top of the page. I am not really finding much to write besides these doodles of broken hearts and tears. Random words come to my mind but no sentences. Fear, pain, hurt, destroyed, lost, betrayed, unloved, alone, helpless, and ruined.

Mark suggested I tell my mom what happened. I don't feel as though I can tell her. I don't want her to be disappointed in me. He said I needed to tell someone with authority. I just don't know what to do, or who to tell. My mom, the police, my doctor, or maybe Dr. Baker?

Just then the phone rang, and I hoped it wasn't Brad. I slowly picked up the receiver and said, "Hello...who's this," not recognizing the number on the caller ID.

"Hey stranger. It's me. Ann. What's up girlfriend?" She sounded overly excited and peppy.

"Oh hey, sis. Are you back from vacation already?" Ann's parents had taken her to Disney over April vacation. "So did you have a blast? Did you remember to kiss Dopey for me?"

"Yeah we had a blast, thank you. But I am glad to be home, I miss your face," she said. I really missed her, too.

Since she has been the one person besides Mark, I lean on in hard times. "I missed you too. Where are you calling from anyway?" I asked.

She responded all cheery, "Mom and Dad bought me a cell phone finally."

Ann and I had been getting closer over the past year. She was like another sister to me, and I to her. I was so grateful for our friendship. I think we would have done just about anything for each other. I was so grateful I met her. She was a good influence in my life. I thought maybe it was time that I hung out with only her, and no more Kelly. I loved Kelly but I felt as though she may not be the best person to hang with all the time. I had all of these thoughts as I paced back and forth in my room.

As I was thinking over the clarity I was having, I realized that Ann had been talking this whole time, I, hadn't even been listening.

"Hey Ann, that's great."

"Wait what, how is that great?" Ann let's out a chuckle.

"What?" Deflecting for a moment I said realizing I had no clue what she was even talking about. Obviously it wasn't something great.

"How is it great that a boy ran by and pushed me in the pool with my clothes on?"

"Oh my gosh, Ann, I am sorry I didn't mean that." I shook my head as I couldn't believe I just said something to make her think that I was listening.

"Amanda? Your not even listening to me are you? What's going on? You are never like this."

I took a breath not wanting to say anything about yesterday. Just distract her. "I'm sorry, I'm fine. I guess I kinda spaced out. But oh my so tell me again what happened? You got pushed in the pool?" As I let out a serious laugh and a sigh. Maybe by me laughing she will not say anything about me acting weird.

"Amanda, I know there is something wrong. What's up? Why are you so distracted? You wanna talk?"

"No I'm good. I'm fine really." I said with a laugh. I want her to think all is hearts and roses. Well I'll let you go. Go get some rest, sounds like you had a long trip."

"Yeah I did. Okay! Maybe tomorrow we can hang out after school?"

"Yeah sound good?"

"Okay we'll talk tomorrow then?" she asked in a worried voice.

"Okay, sounds great. Good night, Ann. I really did miss you,"

"I missed you too, Sis. Sweet dreams." She hung up, but I hesitated before putting down the phone, listening to the dial tone for a minute before finally hanging up.

I decided I would talk to her tomorrow after school, and I would tell her everything. Maybe she could help me figure out what to do.

***

I went through the next day feeling shitty, and depressed, and I actually thought about skipping, but it was the first day back from our April vacation. I had been trying so hard to get my grades up and couldn't really afford to fall behind and possibly miss new lessons. I didn't want to see Brad. I usually didn't as most of his classes took place on the third floor and mine on the first.

As I strolled down the hall to my first class, Algebra, I bumped into Mark. Literally banged right into his back. I'm such a klutz sometimes. I am constantly walking into people and stuff. Tripping over my own feet. I embarrass the hell out of myself. He was talking to someone who immediately laughed, said bye, and took off. I was so embarrassed, I really needed to start paying more attention to where I was going. I was just always distracted or walking with my head down.

Mark looked surprised to see me at school today, but he gave me a huge smile and hug. "Why hello pretty girl. How are you today?" he asked.

I gave him a disgusted face, and said, "Ew, Mark. You totally just sounded like a creepy old man."

He laughed. "Really, I did? Sorry." Then he switched gears to make his voice more feminine. "Hey girl, how are you doing?"

I busted out laughing. "Wow, I don't even know who the hell that was but stop it. I'm fine! And you?"

Laughing he said, "I'm better now that I saw you." He got all serious and asked, "Have you seen Brad yet?"

I rolled my eyes, took a deep breath. "No and I don't wanna see him," I answered. "If you see him tell him to stay away from me."

Mark put his hand on my shoulder. "If I do see him I am gonna do more than tell him that!"

I gave him a side stare that indicated I did not want him to cause a scene. I shook my head and rolled my eyes, then closed them. I took a breath and said, "Mark, please. Not here at school."

He then pulled me into a hug and kissed the top of my head. I rested my cheek on his chest and said, "Please, Mark?"

Pulling away he bent his head down and grabbed my chin, forcing my face to look at his. "I already told you I would lose it if he hurt you and he crossed the line here," he said, with anger and certainty. "He broke you and stole something so precious from you....something that he cannot give back. I'll try and keep my cool but I'm not making any promises. My only promise is to protect you." He started to walk away while I just stood there in complete shock by his willingness to protect me. I shut my eyes and let out a sigh of defeat. I didn't want Mark to get in trouble but I would like to see Brad get what he deserved.

I walked into class, and took my usual seat all the way in the back, not feeling like looking at or talking to anyone. The period seemed to last forever and I found myself dozing off before the bell startled me awake. Quickly I got up and hustled to my next class.

Rushing in, I again took a seat in the back of the room and got my things out for class when I noticed a very tan Ann coming to join me. She sat down in the seat next to me just as the bell rang.

She leaned in close and whispered, "Hey, Sis, what's up?"

I gave her a big smile. "I'm obviously not as good as you, Ann. Look how tan you are. What the hell, did you sleep outside the whole time you were on vacation?"

She chuckled. "No, but my mom and I did lay by the pool one day while my dad played golf."

"I'm so jealous. I wish I could tan," I said, looking down at my own milky white skin. "I just burn to death in the sun, not getting any color except red."

I shook my head, annoyed that everyone else seemed to tan except me.

When the teacher started talking, I was so tired I could barely keep my eyes open. All I wanted was to go home and go to bed. Then I remembered I was going over Ann's after school. My nerves kicked in, and I started sweating, thinking about telling her what had happened over the weekend. I instantly started feeling sick; I wanted to throw up. I asked to go to the bathroom and ran, making it just in time to throw up into one of the nasty school toilet. Oh my nerves were shot. I couldn't wait for this all to be over.

"Are you alright?" Ann whispered when I got back to class.

"Yeah I'm fine, no worries," I told her, but I could tell she didn't believe me.

The rest of the class dragged on, as did every other one after it. Thankfully the bell finally rang and everyone got up and darted out as fast as they could.

I attended my other classes just kinda floating through the rest of the day. I was walking back to my locker when I spotted Ann standing in the hall waiting for me. "What the hell is taking you so long? You are usually zippy to get outta here."

Ann and I were the last two to leave. "Hey, my mom should be here. Are you ready, or do you need to go to your locker?"

I cleared my throat and said, "Yeah I need to go grab a book. Can I meet you out front?"

She smiled. "Of course. I'll see you outside."

I quickly walked to my locker not wanting Ann's mom, Holly, to have to wait for me. Inside, a piece of paper was sitting on top of all my stuff. Someone must have slipped it thru the slots. I grabbed it and unfolded it. All it read was, "I'M SORRY!" in a guy's handwriting. I stood there frozen for a moment, not breathing. I heard someone walking heavily, and it brought me back to reality. I took a deep breath and crumbled it up the note, threw it back into my locker, grabbed my book, and slammed the door shut.

I started shaking and I felt sick again. I shook my head and tried to not think about it. I spotted Holly's car and rushed over to it. "I'm sorry, Holly. My locker got stuck and I couldn't open it so I had to try a few times."

She turned and smiled at me. "No worries, honey. As long as you got what you needed."

Oh yeah, I did. I got way more than what I needed, I thought to myself as I took a deep breath. "I did, thank you!" I said through my teeth.

I wasn't expecting to get a note from Brad. I was hoping for no contact at all. Well I guess I got way more than I needed when he raped me. I shifted uncomfortably in my seat and rested my head on the window, watching the trees whip by as we drove to Ann's house.

Inside, her mom offered us coffee cake that she had made and we gobbled it up almost as soon as she had given it to us. She made the best coffee cake I had ever had. I also hadn't eaten very much of anything the last couple of days.

After our snack, we headed up to Ann's room. Such a beautiful room, where everything matched. Her furniture was white and all the accent stuff navy blue and green. It was also clean, well organized, and super cozy. Nothing like my room with all its mismatched stuff.

Ann turned the radio on and we both sat on the floor to do our homework. She quickly jumped up and said, "I almost forgot. I got you something from Disney!" She walked over to her closet, grabbed a Disney bag, and pulled out a stuffed Dopey and a box. She handed them to me and said, "Here."

"Ann, you did not have to get me anything. But I am so happy you did. Thanks a bunch." After giving Dopey a squeeze, I opened the small box. My heart sank. Inside was a heart-shaped necklace with my name engraved in it. It was so precious; I felt so loved.

"Turn it over," Ann said, and I did. The engraving read: "Best friends 4 Eva, Ann." I looked up at her with tears in my eyes.

"Thank you, Ann. I love it. It's perfect." She bent down and gave me a hug. "I thought it was perfect, too," she said.

When we pulled out of the hug, I realized that I was crying. Chuckling she joked, "Why are crying? It's not that nice."

"You cannot even imagine how much this means to me," I said, fondling the necklace between my thumb and fingers. I couldn't help but to feel overwhelmed by our relationship. I wanted so badly to have a friendship like this for so long, and now I had it. I knew in my heart that our bond was one of a kind. It was the kind of relationship where you just knew that it was right, that it was true.

As I sat there thinking about her friendship and how much it meant to me, I was suddenly hesitant about telling her what happened this past weekend. Ann has always been perfect, good grades, didn't get into trouble. I was afraid she was going to think less of me and I didn't want that. I didn't want her to think I really wanted it, when I truly didn't. I sat quiet for a few minutes.

Ann finally broke the silence. "Amanda, are you okay?" She scooted over and sat next to me. She turned into me. "You can talk to me. Did something happen, while I was away? Did Brad break up with you?"

I sat there and stared at her thinking about what to say. I slowly shook my head, to indicate no. Then I quickly started shaking my head yes. Then I ripped off the band-aid, so to speak.

"Brad raped me." I said it clear enough so she could hear me, but she just kind of sat there in shock for a moment. Then she gasped loudly. Not saying a word yet, she gave me the biggest hug. I think it was harder than the one I got from Mark.

She sat there for a minute while it sunk in. "Oh my god, when did this happen?" she said with concern. "Are you okay? I knew he was no good." She pushed me back to look at my face. I had stopped crying, telling her I had a sense of peace come over me.

I began to talk, telling her briefly, what happened. I didn't really want to get into too much detail because I didn't want to taint her brain, her memory of me. I wouldn't want her to think about it every time she saw me. I don't want any pity.

"Ann I just want to move on from this. I have learned from my mistakes, and I don't intend on dating anymore for a long time. I am turning over a new leaf. No more partying, no more hanging with the older crowd. From now on it's me and you. Homework, sports, studying, strictly school, normal stuff, and simply just being teenagers." I looked at her and gave her a fake smile. She just sat there staring at me. She looked deep in thought. I knew she was trying to think of what to do, how to respond to me trying to push it all away.

"I'm sorry that this happened to you," she said. "But can I ask you something?" She paused for a moment shaking her head and waiting for me to answer. I shrugged my shoulders and gave her a look of uneasiness. Furrowing my brow, I twitched my lips to the left, not saying a word. She knew now that I wasn't sure. "What are you going to do now?" I just shook my head and closed my eyes.

I turned and gave her a wicked grin, one of chalkiness. After a moment I said, "I'll do what I can to make sure that he understands that we are over. I'm gonna tell him that I never want to see him, or his pathetic face again."

I jumped up off the floor and started heading for the door. "I haven't heard from him since it happened on Saturday afternoon." I looked down at Ann. She was still sitting on the floor, looking shocked. So I asked, "What?" while putting my hands out at my sides.

She looked at me with her head turned slightly to the side. "That's it Amanda?" she asked. "What about his consequences? You suffer with all this, but what about him? How does he pay for all this?" she said with a sob.

I just shook my head and rolled my eyes because I myself wasn't sure of the answers. I just knew that at that very moment all I wanted to do was to tell him how I felt. As I started walking out of her room, Ann said, "What are you doing?" She started walking to me.

I shrugged my shoulders and said, "I'm gonna go and use the phone that's in the spare room." She put her arm around me and walked me to the other room.

"Amanda, please collect your thoughts before you speak and don't go easy on him." She then gave me a half smile and turned and walked away.

As I called his house I thought maybe he wasn't home, as it just rang and rang. But after several rings he answered with an irritated "Hello." I hesitated hearing his voice, but then I quickly spoke while I had the nerve. "Hey I just wanted to say a few things," I said as I was shaking profusely.

"Yeah, okay, Amanda. Whatever. Go ahead. Say whatever it is."

I changed my tone to sarcasm and began laying into him. "So first off, I wanted to say thank you for calling me, and making sure I was okay. That was very nice of you. It was also nice the way you played me, used me, hurt me, and lied to me telling me you loved me. Then stealing my virginity. Leaving me broke, hurt, and in pain. You're a lying bastard and I never want to see you again, ever. And if you do see me, for your sake, you had better pretend like you don't even know me. Don't look twice, don't think twice, just go on your pathetic way. I hope you live happy knowing what you so greedily stole from me. You are a giant piece of shit rapist. Karma is a bitch and I hope that it all comes back to you and fucks you hard in the ass. Goodbye, Brad. Have a great fucking life!" then I hung up, slamming the phone down.

As I stood there, I took a few deep breaths. It was a helpful thing to just relax and calm down. Dr. Baker had told me that when I was experiencing high stress, I should take a moment to breathe and relax.

I was so proud of myself. So satisfied with the way I just left that. I prayed this would be the last time I ever spoke of this, the last time I ever spoke to him.

Then I turned to find Ann and Holly standing in the doorway. My mouth dropped open and my eyes widened as I was in shock. Had Ann...told her mom?

Ann cleared her throat and spoke. "Amanda, I am so sorry but I had to tell. You need to do something about this. You can't just let it go like that." She choked back a sob as she watched me drop to the floor.

The next thing I know Ann and Holly are by my side. Ann is just sitting there kneeling on her knees. Holly puts her hand on my head and says, "Amanda?...Amanda, you need to do something about this!"

She comes closer to me, now putting her arms around me. I know they are right, but I don't want anyone to know, especially my mom. Holly is talking to me but I'm not really listening. I hear her talking but its all a blur. I have a million things running through my head. I hear a few distinct words from her mouth. I hear "rape," "STDs," "pregnant," and "your mother." My body is starting to tingle and I am getting lightheaded.

I feel strong hands lifting me up off the floor. I hear people talking. And through my blurry vision I see Jim and my mom. And then things go black.

***

I woke up hearing voices. I started opening my eyes and saw EMTs with their hands on my neck, placing a plastic thing over my face. I could hear them talking and things were now starting to get clearer. I looked around the room at everyone watching over me as I lay on the floor of Ann's spare bedroom.

Ann, Holly, and Ann's dad, David, stood in the far corner, while my mom and Jim stood at my feet. I started to speak and put my free hand to my face when the EMT holding the air to my face said, "Glad to have you back, Amanda. My name is Sam and this Daryl. We will be taking you to the hospital."

I heard my mom gasp; she was a crying mess. I watched Jim console her as she asked if she could ride in the ambulance with me. Everything else until we got to the emergency room was a blur.

My mom was sitting next to me, holding my hand and being very quiet. I wondered to myself if I should say something when in walks a doctor.

"Hello, Amanda. Mrs. Nelson. My name is Dr. Stock and I would like to take a moment to ask a few questions, if that's okay?"

My mom shook her head. "Of course."

I turn my head to the side, looking away from my mom and the doctor as she starts asking me questions. "Amanda, can you tell me what happened?" I just sat there silently, unsure of what to say. "Amanda, the sooner we talk the sooner you can leave," she said.

I knew I didn't want to stay here forever so I started to speak. "I was standing in my friend's spare room and I passed out, I think." I closed my eyes, anticipating the next line of questions.

"Can you tell my why you think you passed out?" the doctor asked kindly.

I took a deep breath. "It's probably because I didn't eat today," I said, then closed my eyes again.

My mom then spoke up. "I got a call from Holly, her friend's mom, asking me to come to her house, cause she wanted to speak to me. When I got there Amanda had just passed out. When that happened I immediately tried to wake her. She wasn't coming to right away so Holly called 911." My mom choked back her sobs.

The doctor continued. "I was stopped in the hall by Holly a moment ago. She told me that you may have something of urgency to tell me," she said.

I whipped my head over to face the doctor. She was tall and thin with long brown hair. "I don't want to talk about it," I snapped. "It's nothing!"

My mom then grabbed my hand. "Amanda what don't you want to talk about? Not eating, have you not been eating?"

"No, Mom. I just don't want to talk about this. Not here, not now."

My mom stood up and leaned over me, holding my face in her hands so I had no choice but to look at her. She spoke now in a stern voice. "Amanda whatever you are hiding, whatever you have to say, you best say it now before I go ask Holly."

I looked at her with frustration. Why wouldn't she just listen to me? I took a big deep breath as tears started rolling down my cheeks. I watched the doctor through my now blurry vision step closer to me. "Amanda," she said with concern, "this is your health and it is important to know all the facts."

As I lay in the bed, blinking back the tears, I took a deep breath and counted to three in my head. Then I blurted it out: "Brad raped me!"

My mother gasped loudly and the doctor rushed to my side.

As I lay there, I shivered from the cold and from the fear that was building up. I tried to remain calm. The next thing I knew, my feet were in these foot holders things as my mother held my hand.

"Amanda I am just going to examine you. Please relax your legs and just breath."

As soon as she touch me I cringed and squeezed my legs together. Whatever she was doing hurt. "Amanda I am sorry I know this is uncomfortable and it soar but you need to relax."

All I wanted was to go and home and go to sleep. When the doctor finished, she told us she was going to have the nurse come in now and take some blood and my mom needed to fill out a paper. As the nurse walked in my mom and the doctor left the room. I felt as though maybe it was better if I didn't have to hear what was going on.

When my mom came back into the room a few minutes later, it looked like she had been crying. The nurse finished labeling the tubes of blood and left the room.

The look on my mom's face was that of fear, sadness, and pain. That is the exact face I did not want to see on my mom. "She told me that we could go home now but we would have to follow up with your regular doctor tomorrow."

As I got dressed, my mom did her best to try and help me. I told her I was fine and pushed her hand away. I then finished putting my shoes on standing quickly to get out of there.

I got dressed and we walked to the waiting room, where Jim was sitting reading a magazine and talking to my dad. Oh shit now he's involved in this? I walked over and asked if we could go, but startled them as they hadn't seen me coming. My dad hopped up quickly from his chair and gave me a big hug. Jim did the same. I pushed from their hug before words were spoken, words I did not want to hear from either of them.

I then turned quickly and walk away. "I just wanted to go home," I said over my shoulder.

The ride home was quiet and awkward. I didn't say a word to any of them. My dad had went back to his house telling me he would see me soon.

As soon as I got home I went to my room and put on comfortable clothes to sleep in. I then climbed into my bed and fell asleep before I knew it. At this point, my mind was blank; it was easy to sleep.

***

I awoke to the sound of my alarm clock going off. I reached over and threw it across the room, smashing it against the wall. At that very moment Jim came rushing into my room. He must have been getting dressed for work. His tie was loose around his neck and his shirt was only partially tucked in. He had a look of panic on his face when my eyes made contact with his. "Are you alright?" he asked with concern.

"Yeah Jim, I'm fine," I replied sarcastically.

"You can stay home from school today if you want. Maybe get some rest. Your mom left for work a little while ago. Your dad called also. He said call him if you need anything," Jim said to me as he came over and kissed my forehead before quietly leaving my room.

He knew that I didn't want to be bothered. It was great that I can now get on with my day and the the heck out of this house, outta this room. I showered quickly and got dressed, threw my hair into a ponytail and jogged out to get the bus. I made it just as the bus just arrived.

I got to school not wanting to talk to anyone. I walked right past some of the people I would usually have talked to, Ann being on of them. I just couldn't right now. I would say all the wrong things and I didn't want to hurt anyone.

When I started to open my locker, I felt a tight grip on my elbow. I immediately froze. I stood there not wanting to turn around. The girl standing at the locker next to me looked at me raised her eyebrows with curiosity and then walked away, slamming her locker shut. The noise from that startled me and snapped me back into the now.

The hand that was gripping my elbow was starting to squeeze tighter and I instantly knew it was...Brad. I turned, quickly ripping my arm from his grasp. As I made eye contact with him I realized he had a black eye. I smirked at the sight of it. He leaned forward placing his arm next to my head while placing his hand flat on the locker to the left of mine. Now I was trapped between the open door of my locker and his arm. Leaning into me, his face mere inches from mine, he spoke to me in an angry tone that made me nervous as shit. "What the hell were you thinking when you told Mark that I raped you?"

I took a deep breath and mustered up my words, when suddenly Brad was no longer standing in front of me. His ass was now sitting on the floor, with Mark standing right behind him. I looked up at Mark. "Amanda you need to just leave. Now!" He demanded between his teeth.

The hall was starting to fill with people. Fuck! They were all standing there watching. I was mortified.

"Mark, not here, not now...Please!"

Mark looked angrily back at me, he was fuming. He then looked down at Brad. "I already told you to stay the fuck away from her," he shouted. Brad started to stand up and say something when two teachers came rushing through the crowd.

Grabbing both Mark's and Brad's arm, they directed them toward the office.

As I let out a huge sigh of relief, I saw Ann walking up to me in a rush. Ahhh! What's next? She started to say something and I just put my hand up for her to stop. I turned on my heel, shut my locker, and walked away. This was something I was not going to talk about at school, with a ton of people still watching.

I headed to the nurse's office and asked her if she could call my mom to come pick me up. I told her that I wasn't feeling very well. There was no way in hell that I was going to stick out this day and have something else go wrong.

When my mom arrived, I didn't say anything to her and she didn't say anything to me. I think she knew that I needed my time.

My plan at home was to take a shower and go to bed early. I needed rest. But first I needed to get some things off my chest. I grabbed my journal and started to write.

Wow the last few days have been a complete cyclone for me. My head has been up and down, left and right, back and forth. I feel mentally and physically drained.

I am meeting with Dr. Baker tomorrow and I will tell him everything, as I know now that I can trust him. I think that I really need him to help me process all this. To make sure that I am handling it well enough that it doesn't cause me any damage. I have had enough of that.

At my appointment I will speak of this for the last time, I hope. Brad deserves nothing, not even a thought.

It's time for me to move on, move forward with my life. This is not what will define me.

I, as of right now, will work my hardest at doing what makes me happy. I will do all I can to achieve my goals in life. This situation is done and over for me. It happened and it sucks very bad, but I am determined to move on. Move past this. Forgive and forget. Forgive myself for taking my life down a path I knew in my heart I shouldn't never taken in the first place. As for forgiving him...I don't think I ever will. Forgetting may happen but it may longer, but I'm sure I will eventually.

***

On my way to my next appointment with Dr. Baker, I felt good about going and wished I could go more often. I felt as though writing in my journal has been helping me so much, as I try to focus and write it all. Things that I found to be helpful to what I call "my disaster recovery."

When I got to his office, I learned he was running a few minutes behind in his previous session, so I sat in the waiting area and read a magazine.

As an older gentleman left his office, the receptionist told me Dr. Baker was ready for me. As I headed to his office, I started to think that the session could go either way; it may help and it may not.

I walked into his office. Before I even sat down, he said, "Amanda you look so tired. Have you been sleeping?" There was pure concern in his voice.

"What? Do I really look that bad?" I asked, all defensive.

"Sorry, Amanda, no. You just don't look well rested or like your cheery self."

I huffed at his response. "Well, a lot has been going on the last few days"

"Just in time to talk about it then. What's been going on Amanda?" He looked at me with complete wonder.

"Well I was raped!" Again I just had to say it. I felt that just blurting it out made it a little easier than taking my time. He gasped and placed his hand on his overgrown mustache. I put my head down and played with a frayed hole in my jeans.

"We really need to talk about this one step at a time. First off, who raped you?"

I sat there silent for a minute as I thought to myself, What is he going to say when I tell him that it was Brad? Is he going to judge me?

"It was Brad!" I blurted as I closed my eyes, put my head down, and went back to the hole in my jeans.

"Oh my, Amanda!" He took a deep breath. "Okay, was this reported? Do the police know?" he asked with sincere concern.

"Well, I am not sure what is going on. I know that the doctor that checked me out at the hospital knows. Her and my mom spoke in the hall for a bit, but I am not sure if there was an official report made or not."

At that moment I started to get really nervous and sweaty, all the while wondering what my life was going to be like once everyone at school found out about this. I could only imagine what they would say. I sat there not being able to think of much else while Dr. Baker talked but I was not paying full attention to him. The next thing I knew our time was up and I was walking out of his office. I had a feeling that things could get bad for me. But for now I wanted to think I could start making progress on putting this all behind me...One step at a time. I would do whatever I needed to do to get past this emotionally, but for me, at this moment, I considered this chapter of my life to be over.

***

My mom ended up pressing charges and Brad spent a year in a corrections facility. I was happy that he got a bit of what he deserved. I hoped that maybe he drops the soap while in there.

Somehow for my sake everything managed to stay relatively quiet. Most people just thought he moved away.

I had ended up speaking to Ann after my appointment with Dr. Baker. I knew I couldn't hold her responsible for something that wasn't her fault to begin with. She was only trying to help. Mark got detention for a couple of days for fighting. I guess he was the one who gave Brad the black eye. I thanked him for sticking up for me, for being there for me when I needed him the most.

I told everyone that knew of this nightmare that I never wanted to speak of it again. It was to stay in the   past   and   I   was   moving   on...

Sophomore & Junior Year

After all I went through when I was fifteen, and all the miserable things from my childhood... I worked hard to put it all behind me, to keep it in the past where I hope it will always stay.

I volunteered the summer after my freshman year at the local teen clinic, which was in danger of being shut down by the city. They no longer could afford to staff and fund the clinic, and they looked to the community for help. I gladly put in regular time there. It was my way of staying connected to the world, helping it run, and keeping it open for young girls who had gone through what I had. I needed to know that there was that place they could go, a place they could get help and be safe.

I started my sophomore year off as a new and happier sixteen-year-old, knowing if I wanted to be happy and do something with my life, I needed to take it one step at a time. I was done with the attitude that it could never be me, that I could not achieve my dreams. I was confident now. I knew to get the things I really wanted I had to bust my ass and simply just do it. I knew that I had to work on my new goal of going somewhere in life. I wanted to be someone who mattered. I wanted to go to college, to love and be loved, and to be happy. I wanted it all.

Dr. Baker really helped me through. Thanks to him, I was able to finally realize that what happened to me in my life was not my fault or my mom's. Sure, my mom made several mistakes and many bad choices, but nobody was going to take me from her. Dr. Baker, gingerly and sensitively, made me see what I had overlooked--the positive changes that had taken place in my life. He and I agreed I didn't need to see him on such a regular basis but he made it clear that if in the event I needed to talk and work things out, that he was there. I will always write in my journal to help me sort through the things in my life.

My family for instance. Everyone was all changing and growing, and moving forward, even though my family was not the traditional family, we were a real family and it was my family. I needed family like I needed water, no matter what and where they lived; family was essential and precious to me. So Dr. Baker convinced me to open up to them. It was an amazing relief.

In doing this, a weight lifted off me. I felt more free from past than ever before. Only my mom, dad, and Jim knew about the rape, though. No one else in my family needed to know. They now knew how I felt. I now had a voice and I was being heard.

With all this new knowledge I gained working with Dr. Baker, I could now see that my past made me a stronger person, and that I would use it to my advantage.

I tried to write daily in my journal, before going to bed. Sometimes I wrote words, lyrics to a great song, or even drew a picture. My journaling was not like it was when I was hurting and trying to heal. It was now more a release of the day. I kept it simple.

The next step I took was to break away from those that did not help me achieve my goals. For me this was breaking the partying relationships with Kelly and the upperclassmen, I didn't want to hurt Kelly, but I had to do what was best for me.

I met Kelly out for lunch one Sunday afternoon and we got to talking a lot about our lives and about the places we wanted to go, and the people we wanted to be. I think this was our first real conversation that wasn't about guys and partying.

"Kelly I have to focus on school and bringing up my grades, but I will always be there for you. I would love if we could still hang out sometimes, but not be to party...I am done with that."

"I understand Amanda, I do. But please know that no matter what I will be here for you always. I want to be better too and not party as much but I love it. I want to live and experience life to the fullest. I don't know maybe seeing you change will make me want to." She chuckled and then changed the subject.

I think she took it pretty well, I think she really understood. We hung out only a few more times before Christmas our sophomore year and then she moved to New Hampshire with her Grandmother. Tragically, her dad passed away unexpectedly at the beginning of December, she had no other family except for her, so she had no other choice but to move. She did stay with Ann and her family while arrangements were made to move. I think the time at Ann's was good for her as she got to see her life and how it could be without the partying.

I was sad for sure that our friendship was ending, but it couldn't last. We did have some good times together but I guess in the end, it was best for both of us. When she moved, we kept in touch sporadically, and she too changed by cracking down and fixing her life.

As for Brad he spent almost a year in a corrections facility, getting out a little early. I was told he left for college out of state. My heart held so much hatred and resentment towards him, I was happy I never saw him again. I had forgiven myself for what happened with him, but not what he did and I would never forgive him for what he took from me, ever.

Mark spoke to Brad once before he left for jail. He told me he about their conversation. Mark told Brad that he hated what had happened, what he did to me. Mark said that Brad insisted that he was sorry and that he never truly meant to hurt me. Saying that he would find a way to make it up someday. Mark told him to just stay far away from me when he got out. I guess Brad said he would, he had no one to blame but himself anyway.

Mark was doing great around this time. He started dating a girl in our class, Julie. They were taking things slow in their relationship; they both felt strongly about wanting to wait until marriage to have sex. I wasn't sure if that was realistic, but I gave him props for wanting to try. It was nice to see Mark happy. I was jealous a bit at times. I couldn't help but think that will never be me. I will never feel happy and be in love. Those things really just felt so far away, so out of reach.

We remained best friends, but given his new relationship, we didn't spend as much time together as before. But we both knew that we were there for each other and that nothing would ever change that.

My mom was finally truly happy at this time. She was working a lot of overtime at the hospital and doing some hours at the local teen clinic where I volunteered. I also tagged along with her sometimes when she worked on the weekends. I enjoyed volunteering there. Not only was I able to spend quality time with my mom, I was also helping others. I felt like what I was doing really mattered at the clinic, even if I was filling the random bowls of condoms that were in the rooms, bathrooms, and around the office, or restocking pamphlets on teen pregnancy, birth control pills, STDs, and rape and abuse. Being there for the local teens was enjoyment enough for me. I was just happy they never closed the place.

My mom was now also saving for a wedding. Jim proposed to her the start of my junior year. It was great to see them so happy and in love. I really look up to them as a couple.

My dad was still happily married to Amy, and my little sister Chloe would be starting kindergarten the next September. Even though I was busy with school and sports I tried to make it over there at least every other weekend, allowing Dad and Amy go out on dates while I'd watch Chloe. We loved watching old Disney movies and doing girly things together, like painting our nails and doing our hair

I talk to my brother on the phone a lot, we tried to talk at least once a week and I'd usually call him every Sunday night. He in turn, would call me either Wednesday or Thursday nights. I've only seen him a few times since he moved away with his mom, but he was happy and doing well. He often flew out to spend time with our dad; usually it's only during school vacations and occasionally a weekend here and there. That's when I usually got to see him. Maybe someday I will fly out there for a visit; his mom had invited me to come anytime.

My sister Samantha is so busy away at school. She is in med school and wanted to be an OB-GYN. Medical school was busy and very time consuming. It was a lot of hard work with all the classes, studying, and internships, she worked part time at a family practice. But we still tried to make time for each other.

Samantha and I, like my other brother and sisters, talked on the phone more than we saw each other. She also came down on vacations and time off as well. She took me to a spa a couple times where we had our hair and nails done. We often went shopping at the mall, caught a movie, or went out to dinner. No matter what we did even if it's just me helping her study or just doing nothing, I still enjoyed being with her. I was so proud of her. She was doing an excellent job with her life. I definitely looked up to my big sister.

Senior's Baby

Oh my god, I cannot believe that high school has gone by so fast. Freshmen year sucked but the rest has been great.

I got and kept my grades up, still not where I'd like to be but I was getting all As & Bs so that was much better than D's and failing.

I worked on issues I carried around, built real relationships with my family and learned how to make the right decisions when it came to my life and my future, with help from Ann. She has been my rock and without her and Holly, I wouldn't be where I was today. They both really pushed me to excel and Ann have even applied to all the same colleges. I was not sure exactly what I wanted to do with my life yet, however, I was thinking about something in the medical field or maybe even psychology, counseling, or something along those lines. Holly and Ann hosted a foreign exchange student from Ireland that year. I thought it was kind of cool that they are doing this. It will be such a great experience for them and the exchange student. She is due to come the beginning of October.

I was so excited for my first day of senior year. I was going to drive in my own new car. My parents, Amy, and Jim, all pitched in and bought me a brand new Honda Civic. They gave it to me last week, on my birthday. I can't believe they got me a car, which they said was an early graduation present.

When I pulled into the school parking lot I spotted Ann's car and parked right next to hers. After I grabbed my bag and got out of the car, a black mustang pulled in the spot next to me. I didn't recognize the car but maybe someone else also got a new one.

"Hey Amanda! Ready for the first day of our senior year?" Ann walked up to me and gave me a hug.

"Yeah were senior's baby!"

The driver emerged from the Mustang. Ann and I just went motionless, not saying a word. The guy that stepped out of the car was so dreamy. Tall and thin but it looked like he had a nice muscular build under his shirt. We both said, "Wow" at the same time.

"Hey girls," he said, walking over to us.

We both looked at each other and smiled, and then, at the same time again, said, "Hi." I couldn't believe how handsome he was. His face was perfect and he had this innocent but bad boy look about him. I reached out my hand.

"Hey. I'm Amanda, and this is my best friend, Ann. Are you new here?"

He flashed a gorgeous smile that could melt a snowman. Shifting from one foot to the other he said, "Yeah, I'm Jason. My family and I just moved here two weeks ago."

I look at Ann, who still had yet to say another word. She like she was meeting celebrity, just standing there with her mouth hanging open and her eyebrows slightly raised. Knowing she wouldn't be speaking any time soon, I said, "Hi

Jason. Welcome to the best high school ever. What year are you in?"

"Senior!"

"Us too," I said. "We're happy to show you around, if you'd like. What's your schedule? Maybe we have classes together."

As he fished through his bag, I elbowed Ann to get her attention. It was pretty clear to me that she was interested in Jason so I decided to keep my distance. Best friends rule.

"My first class is calculus, with Mr. Harvey," he said, looking down at his schedule. "Oh really?" I said. "Well Ann has that same class so maybe she can walk you. Right Ann?" I smiled at her reassuringly.

Ann finally snapped out of it and said, "Umm yeah. Of course Jason. I can show you the way."

"I'm gonna be late for class but l will catch up with you two later. Have a good first day Jason. Have a good one Ann," I said with a vicious smile and a wink and I walked away.

I was excited for this new school year but hesitant at the same time. I wasn't sure what exactly what I wanted to do yet after graduation, and I was a little nervous.

Stopping in the hall after class I spotted Mark and talked to him for a bit. "Hey where the hell have you been the last few weeks stranger?" I yelled out to him as I approached his locker.

"I know I know Amanda sorry I've been busy with work and oh I have a new girlfriend too." He lightly chuckled and shrugged his shoulders.

"Oh really what happened with Julie? Couldn't wait to have sex? I said with a laugh that turned awkward real quick when I noticed the change of facial expression when I mentioned her name. Damn I think I hit a soft spot here.

"Well yeah she did actually!" He said as he looked away. "I guess she really didn't want to wait after all."

"Oh shit I'm sorry, well how about this new girl? What is her name? Do I know her?"

He smiled so big his cheeks must have hurt. "Her name is Stacy and we met at the country club during my second shift there. She's a lifeguard too. I can't wait for you to meet her, your gonna love her. So how was the clinic this summer?"

"It was great. I learned a ton. It was slow a few times so I read like ever pamphlet they had."

"That's great and what about your dad's did you have a good time there? I stopped by your house and your mom said you were at his house for the week. I was gonna come over and visit you there but I decided against it and just wait until you got back."

I was happy that he found a girl. I could see in his eyes that he was truly happy and that made me happy. He was such a good guy and deserved the best. His last girlfriend cheated on him because he wasn't ready for sex. I couldn't understand why she didn't just break up with him. Oh what a slut she was. So we hugged and went on our way. Now it was time for my favorite class, lunch.

Walking to the cafeteria, I got distracted by an underclassman who was walking beside me. She could not have been more than sixteen and she was very pregnant. All I could think was that could have been me. My mind drifted to wonder how she had ended up like that, and I felt bad thinking what if she was raped. Was she was ready to have sex? Had she visited the clinic?

I was pulled from my thoughts when all of a sudden I completely collided into someone. I looked up to find a fellow classmate standing there with a guilty smile on my face. Chris Jenkins. He was a jock, but also one of the nicest guys in the school. And not to mention extremely cute, too. Tall, with light skin, dark blonde hair, and blue eyes. He was also buff from playing sports.

"Oh sorry, Chris! I wasn't watching where I was walking."

"Hey cutie, don't worry about it," he said, with the biggest grin on his face. "Actually, I'm kinda surprised you even know my name, Amanda."

I stood there thinking as I was in shock myself a bit that he even knew my name. Geesh with spending my whole life in my own little bubble and not wanting to let anyone in, with the exceptions of Ann, Mark, Kelly, and maybe one or two other fellow classmates. I haven't even tried to make a connection to my classmates. All I really wanted I guess was to go to school and be done. Yes I wanted to make friends but I never was the one to initiate conversation. This year was feeling a bit different. Maybe I should start trying to know more people. I think I'd like to get to know him. He is my type I have always thought he was a cutie but totally out of my league. Out with it Amanda...go for it was all I could think. Swallowing the lump in my throat then getting it out. "Actually Chris, I'm shocked you know my name."

He was smiling at me but also kind of fidgeting with his bag nervously. He reached out and tugged me over closer to the wall. "Here, let's not get run down again," he said with a devilish smirk.

Instantly my palms started sweating. I couldn't believe he was actually wanting to continue this conversation with me. Me? I tried to make light the situation. "To be honest, it sort of happens to me all the time. Ya know running people down." As a twelve-year-old girl giggle escaped me.

He chuckled. "Well, if I can be honest here, I have always known your name and I have always thought you were cute, klutziness and all. Just to make it even and I can't believe I am going to tell you this but it's been ever since we met in the library back in middle school. I would never forget a face like yours. It's as pure as an angel."

I blushed not knowing how to react and I said, unsurely with yet another chuckle, "Thank you."

Laughing back at me. "See you are cute. You just got embarrassed by me telling you you're cute. Or wait was it cause I called you klutzy?" Standing there staring at me with a side glare and flirty smile.

I sighed not being able to help the fact that I thought he was so handsome leave my head for one moment to even speak. He just stood there and waited for my reply. At the raise of his eyebrow I started to speak. "Well I don't hear things like that too much, so yeah I guess both. No one ever really agrees with the fact that I am a klutz or cute for that matter."

"Well you are! Cute I mean, cute. But I guess the clumsiness can be cute too though sometimes." He smiled widely and rubbed my arm.

His touch on my upper arm sent what felt like an electric current through my body. I could feel my cheeks get red so I bowed my head down and to the side for a moment. He started talking again so I looked back up at him.

"Well, Amanda I'm sorry I have to end this but I need to go out to my car and grab a book before the bell, so I will be seeing you around I guess." He flashed a smile as he adjusted his stance. That one smile sent a wave of even more warmth through me.

I thought he was done and was gonna walk away so I adjusted my bag and put a foot forward to start walking. I smiled back at him and was about to say bye when he lightly grabbed my elbow. "Amanda, do you think maybe we can get to know each other? Ya know, maybe talk sometime?"

I blushed again. "I'd like that," I said and started walking away with much excitement. And now that I was in a good mood. I was on a mission to find Ann to tease her about Jason.

I spotted her at our table and went to join her. "Hey, Sis, what's up?" she looked up at me and I knew she was thinking about Jason. As I got out my lunch, I said, "You like him don't you?"

She smiled at me while scanning the room, most likely looking for him. "Amanda, he is so handsome and dreamy."

I smiled back at her now really beginning to bust her balls. "Well, I could tell that you were struck by his hotness. You didn't even talk when he introduced himself." I took a sip of my water and said, "You just stood there with your mouth on the ground. Do you need to go home and change your panties?"

She blushed. "Ewww, Amanda. You're so gross."

I cracked up laughing. She was so shy when it came to guys and sex talk. "Well it's true. Anyone could tell you wanted him. It was written all over your face. Did he ask you out yet?"

"I don't think he will," she said, first looking down at her food then back to me.

"I saw how he looked at you. He wants you as much as you want him. I bet he asks you out by the end of the week!" I said.

She chuckled "You're on! What are the stakes?"

"Ah! A challenge!"

"Well, I saw you talking to pretty-boy Chris after your klutzy ass walked right into him," she said with a laugh, then paused for a moment before she challenged: "If Jason doesn't ask me out by Friday then you have to ask Chris out."

I smiled and thought, Well he kind of already asked me out. "Deal," I said. "But as for you, if Jason doesn't ask you out, then you have to ask him." I think I just confused her but either way, everyone wins.

I said to her, "Ann for the last 3 years, we have done nothing but study and bust our asses. This year we only have this term to take classes that we actually need credits for, then after that, it's slacking off until graduation. So let's do it. Let's experience some new things this year. Maybe date a bit, go to the movies, and kiss a couple of boys or something, I don't know. We are going off to college soon. We at least need to know how to talk to a guy and maybe for you if your lucky get to know how to kiss a guy?"

She huffed as if she was upset by me calling her out then said, "Fuckin deal, bitch."

"I can't believe you just swore!" I laughed. "And you called me a bitch? Really?"

We burst out laughing until I noticed Jason coming over to our table. "Oh, hey, Jason. How's your first day?" I asked.

Ann stopped laughing right away and was all embarrassed until he said, "Please don't stop laughing. I love your laugh. It's so cute and kinda sexy!" Her face turned ten shades of red. It was great.

I decided to leave them alone. "Here, Jason," I said, standing and offering him my chair. "I am done here."

He took my chair, keeping his eyes on Ann, but not looking like he knew what to say. I decided to give them something to talk about. "So what class do you have next, smarty pants?" I asked Jason.

He smirked at me and said, "I don't know let me check. I think it's...umm."

I nodded at Ann. I had a feeling in my heart, and I think she did too that, he would have the same class as her, Anatomy and Physiology.

He looked up from his schedule. "I have A&P next," he said, and I tried not to laugh.

"Oh good," I said, "then you can walk Ann, because she has that next too. Look at that. Almost all the same classes," I said. "Looks like it was meant to be." I ducked away before Ann got a chance to smack me.

When I walked into my next class, bio, there was Chris sitting in the back, right where I would sit. I smiled and bravely took the seat next to him.

"Hey cutie, you just completely made my semester by walking through that door," he said as I sat down.

I pulled open my bag to get out my pen and notebook and said, "Oh same to you. I mean umm, I, oh hell, you know what I meant."

He lightly chuckled and said, "Come on, please don't stumble on your words. You don't need to be nervous when you talk to me. Just relax and be your cute little self."

Smiling, I took a deep breath. "Really ,Chris, how do you know that I stumble on my words, and that I'm nervous?" There it was again, that smile. He made me feel so warm with that smile.

"Without sounding all stalker-like, and I'm sorry if this does..." He paused for a minute to slightly shake his head, then placed his hand on his forehead. "Like I said earlier, I have always thought you were cute. I know who you are, probably more than you think I do."

"Chris it's no biggie really." I was trying so hard to play it cool I really was I just didn't realize that he really probably knew me more than I thought. "I just am not..."

"Alright everyone, let's get this class started. Enough talking for now you can all get back to your chatter later." Oh perfect time as the teacher cuts me off.

The end of the class came fast. It must have seemed that way anyway because I was in such a daze throughout the whole class. All I thought about was Chris and about the few meetings or classes we've had together. I looked over at Chris a couple of times discretely and both times he looked away quickly. I kept focus on the teacher the rest of the time or doodled on the paper on my desk. Looking up to the clock I still couldn't believe the class was over already. Did they shorten that block?

Then out of nowhere, Chris said, "Funny I was thinking the same thing."

"What? Sorry what did you just say?" I asked him, confused.

"That they shortened the block. I was thinking that too. It did go by pretty fast."

I was so embarrassed. I didn't even realize that I had spoken aloud. He didn't seem to notice my embarrassed state. Instead, he handed me a piece of paper and said, "So here's my number."

I looked at him and he had this captivating, huge but beautiful smile on his face. I blushed and I said, "Chris let me give you mine too because I could probably get overly eager and call you too quickly." I wrote down my number and handed it to him. As I packed up and started to walk away, he called my name.

I only just then realized we were the only ones left in the room. "Yeah?" I said.

He walked quickly over to me and now he was toe to toe with me. I looked him in the eye and noticed something different in the way he was looking at me. Next thing I knew his face was mere inches from mine. Then he blurted out: "I can't believe this is happening right now. I can't explain it but, I want to kiss you so bad. I almost actually did earlier in the hall."

I have no idea what came over me at that very moment, because next thing I knew my lips were on his. They were so soft. His tongue pushed between my lips, opening up my mouth to him, and our tongues began stroking and twisting together, sending a tingly feeling through my whole body. Besides that fact that the kiss was hot, thoughts were running crazy through my head. We literally only talked for the first time that day since middle school and now we were kissing--and it doesn't feel awkward... That it feel s deeper than it should...

Senior year was going to be a challenge for Ann and me, with what we might be in for with these two boys.

Dating Chris

I was sitting on the floor in my room doing homework when the phone rang. I looked at the caller ID when my phone showed it was Chris my heart almost beat right out of my chest. I tried to contain my nerves when I answered the phone with the calmest and sweetest, "Hello?"

"Hey, cutie. It's me, Chris. So I know that there is some kind of rule or code out there in regard to calling someone, but I never really understood all that so they don't fly with me."

"It's okay. I don't mind. I think that stuff is all shit if you ask me. So what's up?"

"Good! So I was wondering if maybe you might wanna go out sometime, get to know each other better. We can do whatever even if it's going to study at the library or go out for coffee or ice cream. Whenever you want just let me know."

"I'd like that. Maybe we can go on a double date or something. Ann has this new kid Jason that she's into and I know he's gonna ask her out. I think it would be good for us all. If that's cool with you?" I waited for his turn down as he must just think I am lame for even suggesting that.

"Oh yeah definitely that sounds good...double date, I like it. Yes you can make the arrangements and let me know when."

What relief I had in know he is cool with it. "Okay, let me call Ann and talk with her and I will let you know tomorrow at school?"

"You can call me back too, ya know. I don't mind."

"Alright if I have an answer I will call you back tonight then." The giant smile that was plastered on my face at that very moment was that of one who may have just won the lottery.

"Okay. And if she's not into it we can always go at it alone, and do a date just you and I if you want that is? But you call her and I will talk to you later." A moment of pure silence then, "Amanda are you still there?"

Clearing my voice, "Yeah yeah sorry I'm here. Yeah that works too. Call you later?Bye!" breathing in deep I waited for his response.

"Yup okay. Good luck. Talk to you soon then. Bye!"

I hung up the phone. I am in awe that this conversation just happened. I can't believe I got asked out on the first day of school. I knew I couldn't waste any time; I needed to call Ann right away.

She picked up after a few rings. "Hellloo!" she answered with mega enthusiasm.

"Why helllooo to you too! What's up why so chipper?"

"Well at the end of the day walking to my locker Jason approached me and asked me out sometime." She was laughing like a school girl. "And guess what? As soon as I decide on what and where, we are gonna go out."

"Well isn't that just perfect 'cause I have your what and where to make it happen. Haha!"

"Wait what? You what?" she replied with the utmost excitement.

"Yes, well, Chris called and asked me out, and I suggested that we go on a double date. I knew that Jason would ask you so I figured it would just be a matter of time."

"Oh my gosh, oh my gosh...Really? Yes let's do it...Let's do a double date." She let out a shriek and said, "Now okay. So when, when do we go? Where do we go?"

"We should definitely make it for a Friday or Saturday night. We can go to a movie or dinner or whatever."

"Yeah I love it! Let's do it this weekend or next weekend then."

"Okay I will call Chris and you call Jason. Lets do it next Saturday night that way we have time to talk about and plan it all out fully."

"Yeah good idea. That way I can work on my parents too," she said with a nervous snicker.

I was sure she thought her parents wouldn't let her, but I was also sure all would be fine. She had to start dating at some point. "Okay, Ann. Maybe turn down the excitement when you call Jason. No giggling like a school girl." I laughed hard when I heard her go silent.

"Not funny, Amanda, I'm not that bad. Well okay, maybe a little. But really am I?"

"Ann, it's okay. Your fine. Now go call him." I responded with a laugh.

"Okay! Alright! Deep breaths." She took a few breaths. "We got this. Go call Chris. Next Saturday it is...My first date!" Laughing then silence. She just hung up on me and didn't say bye? Really? She's that eager? I thought while laughing and hanging up the phone.

I couldn't call him right now. Yes codes and rules, I needed to wait a little while.

I went to get a drink then came back and called right away. Yes I guess I was eager too!

Chris and I did hang together at the library a few times in the couple of weeks leading up to our date, just getting to know each other with no pressure. We talked about little things and big things. We learned we had so much in common. But the pressure did come the day of the big date. We had only kissed that one time at school, so I knew that it was going to happen that night.

Ann and I got ready at my house. I was wearing a pair of skinny jeans and a black flowing top with a long beaded necklace and a pair of wedges. Ann had on something very similar ,although she ditched the necklace and wedges and wore just flats. Needless to say, that Ann and I looked kinda hot. We sat on the front steps waiting for the guys to pick us up. We had arranged for Chris to pick up Jason, then us.

As we sat and waited Ann and I didn't say much to each other. I think we were both way too nervous to talk. I went to say something when I heard a horn and the sound of tires pulling into my driveway. We both looked at one another and smiled. We simultaneously stood from the steps and looked over to Chris's car in the driveway. "Here we go!" I said.

We were all smiles as walked down the few cement steps of my house. We paused briefly as we heard the car doors close. I smiled at the site of Chris. He had on a pair of dark washed jeans and a black polo shirt. Jason had jeans and a t-shirt with writing all over the front. They were both polite and respectful. Our first dates were going to be great. I just know it.

As the guys approached us oddly they both were doing the same thing, lightly shaking there heads and grinning from ear to ear. I had a strong suspicion that they must have liked what they saw. Well it was just that until I heard a whistle come from one of them. I wasn't sure which one had whistled because I was carefully watching my every step. I was wearing a larger heel than my standard Converse sneakers. Somehow I actually managed to walk all the way to him without falling flat on my face. A record for me!

"Wow don't you girls look mighty fine today?" Jason said with a wicked grin.

"They most certainly do. And Amanda I am proud of you. You made it all the way down the steps without tripping," Chris said with a laugh.

Smacking his arm "Chris, you're not supposed to say anything. Now you just jinxed me!" I laughed right back at him.

We got into the car, Chris and I sitting up front and Jason and Ann in the back. I looked into the back seat and felt bad for Ann. Her nerves were way worse than mine. I know she was super nervous by the way she sat. Not only with her legs turned in toward him trying to use her legs to keep him at a distance but she was as far on her side as she could possibly go. Jason got in and his legs were so long that they took up more than just his side but his knee was closer to her side, almost touching her. Ann straightened out and sat with her hands on her lap. She gave me a nervous smile. When Jason put his hand on hers and started talking to her, she turned to face him. She was too cute. So red! I laughed and turned to Chris as he started to drive us to the restaurant.

He turned to me, "Hey!" he said, with a nod and a smile then focused back to the road.

"Hi!" I managed to get out a moment later.

Within minuets we arrived at this little Mexican restaurant on Main Street. Chris and Jason both promptly got out of the car, opening the doors for us. They were both polite and respectful.

We were seated in a booth right away by a man wearing a large sombrero. We all placed our order. While we waited for our dinner to arrive we snacked on tortilla chips and salsa, Chris and I made small talk with Jason to make him feel comfortable. "How do you like it here so far?" I asked him.

"I love it," he said. "The town is so historic and beautiful. The ocean is amazing and the people are all so nice here." He smiled as he turned to look at Ann.

"Yeah, everyone in this town are all very caring and loving people. The historic sites are something else. Each one has so much behind it."

"I would love to show you around sometime and tell you about them if you want." Ann finally spoke up.

"I would love that," Jason said with enthusiasm.

The waiter with the large sombrero served us our dinner and told us in Spanish to enjoy. "Por favor disfrute." I had taken spanish for a couple of years so I understood a little. Actually, Chris and I had been in the same Spanish class last year, he only class we had together since freshman year.

"Gracias Señor!" Jason replied in perfect Spanish.

"Dude, you speak Spanish?" Chris asked curiously.

"A little," Jason responded, reluctantly.

"Wow, man that's cool. I take Spanish but I suck at it." Chris stated. As we all laughed at his confession.

I can just tell that these two will get along just fine. Talking minimally over dinner we finished and all decided to go to the movies.

As we exited the restaurant Chris placed his hand on the small of my back while he pushed opened the door with his other hand. "Did you enjoy your fajitas?"

"Yes, I did thank you very much. And did you enjoy yours?" I asked in return.

"I sure did. Best ones I've ever had. Thank you for coming out with me tonight." While he put his arm around my shoulders, I smiled at him and rested my head on his shoulder.

"I am so happy you asked me out," I confessed to him not even thinking before I spoke.

Chuckling, he said, "Well, since we are confessing here, I am thrilled to get to know you. I am more than happy that I asked you out. I love to see a smile on your face. And since I brought up your face and smile now I guess would be a good time as any to tell you how beautiful you look tonight."

I blushed at his compliments. "Thank you Chris! You don't look too bad yourself."

We stopped when we arrived at his car. Ann and Jason had stopped walking and were talking back near the restaurant. They were facing each other and he was holding her hands. I turned back to look at Chris and he was leaning against his car legs crossed at his feet and arms folded lightly over his chest. "So, you're having a good time so far? Do you really want to continue this date and go watch a movie with me?"

I walked over closer to him. "Yes of course I do. I want nothing more than to finish this date off with a romantic movie."

"Wait...wait ...Romantic? No no no, No romantic movies. If I see kissing of any kind I want to see me kissing you again."

As I stepped closer he reached out and grabbed the loops of my jeans and pulled me close. I gave in and just kissed his soft lips. When his tongue collided with mine it sent a volt of heat through my entire body. We broke off to the sounds of Ann clearing her throat. We smiled at each other as he opened the door for me. We got in the car and continued on our date at the movies. We held hands through it only kissing twice briefly when it started and when it ended. He dropped us off at my house. We all got out of the car and sat on the steps of my house.

"So, Amanda, did you really have a good time? Or are you just saying that to shut me up?"

"No, I had a great time tonight. Thank you! I think we should do it again sometime."

We managed one last kiss for the night before it was time for me to get in to meet my curfew.

This was all new too me, and after just a few weeks together, it felt so right and normal. The four of us had double-dated a couple of times over the next two weekends leading up to our date alone.

It was a Saturday, late morning at the beginning of October; we had been dating for about a month. He was coming to my house to pick me up. I got up so early to shower, eat, do my makeup and hair, and find something to wear. As I sat on the couch waiting for him. I was overly anxious about our date as it has been all I've been thinking about since he told me last week about it. Basically he had told me that our first real date alone was going to be amazing. So needless to say I'd been thinking about the endless possibilities the day could have.

I thought back to our conversation about it again wondering if maybe I missed a clue somewhere.

"I've planned an entire day and it's all a surprise," he'd told me. "We're going to have a ball I am sure of it. You may want to bring your camera."

"Awesome I can't wait. But I don't have one. It broke."

"Well that's okay. I will bring one," he'd said before giving me a tight hug and a soft kiss goodnight.

A knock on the door brought me back to reality. I jumped right up. I could not wait any longer for this date to start.

Opening the door I find him standing there with a small bouquet of flowers and that smile that just warmed me instantly.

I smiled back at him and welcomed him in. "Those daisies are beautiful=. Let me put them in water and let my mom know we are leaving."

He walked over to the kitchen with me. "I have this for you, too." He held out his hand to me. When I looked down to see him holding a disposable camera.

I was confused about the camera for a moment. "A disposable camera? What in the world is this for? To take pictures of my dinner?"

"No. Remember you'll want this to capture all the memories from only one of the best days ever."

I thought that was just so cute. As I smiled at him he winked at me. "Oh yeah that's right." I set the vase on the counter then turned to the incoming voice of my mother walking into the living room.

"Now what are you two up to today?" she asked while walking over to the coffee pot.

"Well, Ms. Nelson, the day is all a surprise. But we are going to dinner in Boston."

"A surprise? Amanda is actually not fighting you about that? She hates surprises!"

"Mom, don't worry about it. I can handle them once in a awhile." I said with a fake smile at her kinda telling her to butt out.

"Oh really? She hasn't put up a fuss about it yet set aside a little begging." Chris chuckled.

"Begging? I think not, no begging i'm cool with it. Next time I may have to beat it out of you. Now maybe we should get going."

"Yeah don't want to miss the train."

"We're going on the train? Not driving?" I asked, puzzled.

He walked over and put his arm around my shoulder. He leaned in and whispered, "Nope! I want our day to be all about you...us. No having to deal with masshole driving or the fuss with finding parking. It's all about you babe," he said with a flirtatious smile.

On the train we talked about family, mostly his as I wasn't really ready to divulge my history yet. I kept my stuff very basic. It was great to learn about his family, I wanted to know everything about him.

"I have an older brother, Ryan. He's in college right now so I don't see him as often as I'd like. He lives almost five hours away."

"That is tough. I know my older sister, Samantha, is in college but she isn't that far away. She visits when she can. What about your parents?"

"Well, my mom and dad have been happily married for twenty-two years. My mom is a part time nurse, but she mostly volunteers her time at the hospital and clinics. And my dad, he's a doctor."

It was great that we had all these doctors and nurses in our lives. "Cool. So our parents must know each other. Well, our moms at least."

"We seem to have many things in common, don't we?" he asked.

"Yeah, actually we do. Didn't you say before when we were at the library that maybe you wanted to be a doctor too? One more thing we have in common. We both want to be able to help people."

"Yeah I think doing research, though," he said. "I'd love to do oncology and help discover a cure for cancer."

When we arrived at North Station in Boston, I could not hold it in anymore so I had to ask, "Chris, come on what are we doing today?"

"I told you, it's a secret. You'll have to wait and see."

I gave him a sad puppy dog face. "I really don't like surprises but I guess I will have to wait and see then." I give him a big cheesy smile back a to try and convince him.

He looked slightly disappointed. "Okay," he said, but he seemed as though he was deep in thought.

So I grinned at him with a flirty smile. "Well, you really don't have to tell me if your gonna be sad about it. Keep it to yourself. That's fine I guess."

He then smiled happily. "No no. I will tell you. I don't want to start our relationship off with secrets. First we are going to a Red Sox game."

I was completely amazed by him already. "A Red Sox game? Really?"

"Yes, cutie and I have something for you that I almost forgot about," he said excitedly.

"What? There is more than the game?"

He removed his backpack and took out a bag, which he handed to me. I opened it to find a pink and navy blue Red Sox shirt. I couldn't believe he had gotten me a gift.

"What really? Why did you do this?" I asked him. "I mean, thank you, but really this is all too much." I don't know maybe it was because he just sprung part of his plan on me then gave me an unexpected gift but I was feeling a bit overwhelmed for sure.

He looked stunned and I felt bad. I shouldn't have freaked out like that, but his generosity was not something I was used to. "Chris, I'm sorry, there is just a lot about me that you don't know. And it's just, I'm sorry. I can't even go into details about me, with you. This is crazy. I have to go home, I'm sorry. I don't want you to think I'm being ungrateful. I'm just feeling overwhelmed." I closed my eyes and took a shaky breath to try and hold back my tears. I started to bolt but he stopped me.

"Amanda no, Stop. Please. I'm sorry. Let me explain something to you."

I turned toward him with a tear in my eye and man did I feel like the stupidest person on the planet. In two steps he was in front of me, reaching his hand up and wiping the single tear that slipped out. I didn't want to cry it just happened.

"Amanda, it's me. I should be the one apologizing to you. I'm sorry," he said, rubbing his thumb over my check to wipe the stray tears that had fallen. He lifted my face to look at his. "I should have just explained my intentions and my plans with you. It's just that I really wanted to surprise you, not make you upset. My dad works for the Red Sox. He is one of their private doctors, and the tickets were free. He offered the tickets to me, and said to go have fun with one of the guys. Then I remembered that time at the library when you told me how much you love the Red Sox, but have never been to a game. Well, that's why you're here. I wanted to share your first game with you." He had the most sincere look in his eyes and spoke to me in such a calm tone.

I stood there feeling like an even bigger fool now for getting all worked up. He dropped his hand to his side. Maybe he was trying to looked relaxed as he waited for me to think about all he had said. I turned my head to the side and watched people pass, but he continued talking. "So, I know that this is going to sound weird, I know that we are young, and that we really haven't known each other personally for a long time, but the way I feel when I am with you, even when we are just sitting, not talking just studying, it's just something I can't explain but there is something very real and strong between us. Our first kiss....Amanda? I know it and I think that you know it too but you are scared."

Placing his hands back on my face so that I would look at him he continued, "Amanda I'm scared too, ya know. I have plans, you have plans, and we'll be graduating before we know it. But I think that we owe it to ourselves to not hold back on those feelings just because we are afraid. I want you to think about this but not now, okay? Let's just have a good first real date, and if you feel later that we don't have anything here and it's all just me, than we can move on. But let's enjoy today, please."

I could feel that all he was saying was true, and I knew because of what I'd been through, I was scared to be hurt, to let him in. But I decided to take a chance and see where it brought us. I'd worked so hard on myself and I knew I owed it to myself to try to be happy. At that moment, I believed he could make that happen, and I decided to go with my heart on this one.

We walked down the street to this little restaurant and were seated without waiting. Once we were seated and opened our menus, Chris said, "Hey, let's take a picture!" He got up and slid into the booth next to me. He held up his camera and snapped a picture of us, and we both laughed, realizing he'd probably chopped our heads off in it.

The waiter saw us struggling with the camera and offered to take a photo for us. Chris leaned into me, putting his right arm around my shoulder, his left hand on my thigh. I froze. The waiter snapped the picture then placed the camera back on the table. We ordered and he left.

Chris's hand was still on my thigh and I felt a weird sense of calm with him just touching me. He patted my leg then reached across the table, sliding his water over. "I'm staying on this side," he said.

Being there with him, I had an overwhelming urge to be honest with him. As I watched him dip a roll into the olive oil and savor it, I spoke his name. He smiled.

"I wanted to tell you... There is a lot about me that I have tried so hard to forget. I have had a very troubled past, and I try and not let it define me. I don't like to talk about it either; I wanted to tell you that little bit so you would know. There are some things that I won't talk about, ever; actually, I'd rather do without it all, completely. I have worked hard to forgive and forget." I took a sip of my water then continued. "I do feel a strong connection with you. I get it all, and I do, I feel it too. Please know, I appreciate your thoughtfulness today and always." I started fidgeting with my napkin on my lap.

He turned to me and took my hand. He looked at me with his big blue eyes. "Well it's good that you told me this, because I have been making myself crazy just wondering why you only open up a little," he said. "It's totally fine with me when, and if, you decide you want to talk. I am here for you either way. I like you enough to trust that you are keeping it in the past for a good reason. We all have secrets. The thing about secrets is that is what they are, so if you feel you need to keep them to yourself, I am fine with that. I will not push or pry. We can take it at your pace, when, and if, you're ready to open up. It is your choice," he said, then placed his other hand on mine, stroking my hand with his thumb. He then leaned in and kissed me on the cheek.

A wave of relief came over me. He understands...I think? Well he's not headed for the door, not yet. So I guess we're good...

We ate lunch in a calming silence. Near the end of our meal I realized I should probably talk to him. I don't want him thinking I am unhappy or have nothing to say. "Chris I just wanted to say thank you for everything so far. Lunch is very tasty and this shirt is pretty kick ass too. Then the game on top of it all. I am excited to be catching my first game with you."

Chris went to say something when he looked down at his watch that's when he realized we needed to get over to Fenway because the game would be starting soon. We made it just in time for the first pitch.

We had a great time. I enjoyed my first game; we took tons of pictures, and had many laughs. I was so comfortable with him. Just being with him made me feel better about myself. He told me a few times how cute I was and really liked me in my new Red Sox shirt. He also told me that he really liked this side of me. He said he liked me being casual, smiling and laughing. He made me feel special, which was so good for me.

The Sox won and we had a great victory train ride back home with all the other amped fans. I was exhausted though. I couldn't stop yawning. He drove me home from the train and walked me to my door.

"I had so much fun today and you definitely surprised me and made it that much better with when you sprung on me some of those random facts about the Sox you knew. I really am amazed that you know as much as you do."

He leaned in and gave me the most passionate kiss I had ever had. As soon as our lips touched my whole body started to tingle and my heart started to race.

When we broke apart from our little make out session "Honestly Amanda I really had so much fun today. Your laughing and smiles of true happiness is what made the game tonight."

"Really me? Not the win?" I asked with question and a yawn.

"Yes really! You should get in and get some rest. Do you wanna do something tomorrow? Maybe go bowling or something?"

"Yeah. Call me in the morning."

"I will," he said, giving me a kiss on the forehead. "Okay, now go get some sleep. I will talk to you later."

I gave him a peck on the cheek. "Thank you for today. I'm sorry again for getting all crazy on your ass." I said as I laughed out loud trying to make light of my stupidity. I turned to walk away and tripped. Catching myself and instantly laughing so hard I thought I could pee. I shook my head in disbelief that I can't even manage my own feet. Chris had grabbed my arm and helped me balance.

"Hey you all right?"

Still laughing at myself I managed to open the door without knocking myself out or anything. "Yeah I'm fine. See leave it to me to trip on nothing." Laughing now almost deliriously I smiled "Goodnight Chris!" and shut the door. Resting my back against it then plopping my head back to the door in disbelief as to the outcome of my date.

***

The following week, Ann's exchange student arrived from Ireland, so things were a little crazy. I helped her with the final touches for Sarah's room. We wanted to make it like home for her; we taped up a couple of pictures of some scenery from Ireland and put green throw pillows on the bed that Holly had made.

After her arrival, we all talked and got to know each other. We showed her the bathroom, she took a long shower, after all, she did have a long flight, and I think she said it was over a 7-hour flight from Dublin. She is cute and very kind, everyone at school will like her for sure. She got out of the shower and asked if we could help braid her hair. We had some fun. We braided each other's hair for the next day of school. We all looked cute. We had Holly take a picture of us.

The next day we went to school and she went with Ann to all her classes, Ann loved it, all she talked about during that first week was that she too wanted to go to Ireland to visit, to see what it would be like.

After talking with her mom and dad, they said that she could go. The school had to make all the arrangements with the school in Ireland, and her parents bought her ticket, she was now all set. She was going back with Sarah, when she leaves to go home in two weeks. Oh no, what will I do while she is gone, I don't want to be alone. I've never been without her for more than a week. Only once, for five days when she went to Disney. I mean even when I stayed at my dad's for a couple weeks we saw each other. We took Chloe to the aquarium and once to the movies. Now she will be leaving for two weeks.

The night before Sarah and Ann were to leave for Ireland, Ann's parents took us all out for Chinese.

It was so delicious and we all talked about their upcoming trip. It was a bittersweet moment for me, I was happy that she was going but I was sad she was leaving me. I think that Chris noticed my hesitation with Ann leaving without me.

Chris leaned in and whispered in my ear, "Don't be sad. I will be here with you. We can spend every day together, if you want." He tenderly kissed my cheek. I pulled back from him, and gave him the biggest smile. He knew that I was happy with that. He had a way of just reading my mind sometimes.

"Amanda do you want to go back to my house? It's still early, only 7:30."

"Sure!"

When we got there, his parents were not home. "I forgot they were at a meeting for hospital funding. Wanna to watch a movie?"

I thought it was great what his parents were doing, it inspired me. I think it inspired him as well because he too wants to be in the medical field, not to mention that it hit a weak spot with my mom, it being the place she too worked. Our parents actually got together one night and had a double date of their own. Our mom's had in fact, worked together a few times before, so they already knew each other.

When we got inside, he said, "Babe go find something to watch and watch. I will make us some popcorn."

I went down the hall to their movie room, and picked a movie and sat on the couch. He came in a few minutes later; he put a movie in, and sat next to me. While the previews were playing, he started talking about us spending time together while Ann was gone. He talked about all the things we could do. As I sat there listening to him talk all I could think about was that he makes me so happy. I could see in his facial expressions and just knew that he was happy too. The excitement was all over his face. It then hit me like a ton of bricks, he really likes me.

I had stopped listening to him anyway after he mentioned something about volunteering again in the pediatric section at the hospital. Then all I could think about was maybe I was almost ready to be with him. I was falling in love. I mean, he was perfect for me. That's when the urge hit me. I practically jumped on top of him mid-sentence. I was straddling him on the couch I searched his eyes while he mine. I lowered my face slowly to his and started tenderly kissing him. His hands were on the bottom of my back resting right above my butt.

He picked me up slightly and guided me to the couch. We faced each other as we lay making out. After a few minutes of intense kissing he put his hand on my right breast. I started to melt at his light and gentle touch. I made almost a low moan, and he pulled back slightly and asked, "Is this okay?" I took him back to my mouth and just kept kissing him, not saying a word.

There was something inside of me that really wanted this more than anything. Things were just so different with him. I was melting at his touch but I also had a hesitant feeling. At the very same moment we stopped.

We both froze and searched each other's eyes again. I think at that very moment we both realized that this was not the time or the place for this. "I don't want this to go any further tonight. Not here, not now. I don't want this for you," he said.

With relief I said, "I was thinking the same thing. Well the part about not wanting this for me because I think I really want this. I think I'm almost ready." He bent down and kissed me with the most unbelievable passion, and I melted into him a little more.

I couldn't believe how I was feeling as he drove me home. I was excited, nervous, and just thrilled that he felt the same way as I did.

We got to my house the same time as my mom. Being kind of spacey, I didn't even realize she was in front of us the whole time. We both smiled and waved to her as she walked to the front door.

We sat there silent for a moment and then he turned to me and said, "Amanda, I have fallen in love with you." I was in shock I think, I sat there with my mouth dropped open until he leaned in and kissed me.

Placing his hand on the side of my face, he kissed me with so much want and passion and I knew I felt exactly the same way as he did, there was no doubt about it. It was then I realized that I was in love and the guy I was in love with, was in love with me. This was real.

"Me too," I said. Then together at the very same time we said those three little words, "I love you!"

I kissed him again and quickly got out of the car, not wanting anything to ruin that moment. When I got inside the house, my mom and Jim were already asleep. I crept into her bedroom, bent down, and kissed her forehead. She stirred a little and said, "I love you, honey. I hope you had a good night."

I headed to my room and changed. I brushed my teeth and got into my cozy bed. A few minutes later the phone rang. I answered it right away not wanting to wake my mom. I thought it was going to be Ann calling back but it wasn't.

"Hey, cutie. I just had to call and say goodnight and I had a good time tonight."

I wasn't expecting him to call. I thought maybe he would have got home or down the street before he realized what he just said to me. I thought it would be Monday at school before I spoke to him again.

"Thanks, I had a nice time, too. Though I have to be honest. I didn't think I would hear from you again until Monday."

I heard him take a breath. "What? You must know me better than that. I can't stay away from you even if it's only just getting to hear your voice. You do realize that there hasn't been a single day that we haven't at least talked on the phone. Amanda not one day since the first night you called me to confirm our first double date, it's been almost 3 months."

Wow, I haven't even thought about that, it's true though. "You are right Chris, I didn't even think about it. I am so happy with you, I didn't think I would ever be happy but then my stupid ass walked into you and now look at us where in love." I giggled lightly.

He gave a long happy sigh. "Yup and this is just the start of it I am sure. But I don't want to keep you, you're probably already in bed. Goodnight, honey. I will talk to you tomorrow. Maybe I will pick you up for lunch."

"Okay, we will talk tomorrow. Sweet dreams." Smiling widely I hung up the phone, and thenI lay in my bed reflecting and writing.

On this day I am so happy. Our relationship took a huge step. I am beyond elated, never did I think I would come this far, find love and be loved and I am finally happy with my life now. I want to take it slow with him but at the same time I feel so much desire for him it hurts.

Eager Cowboy?

The weeks without Ann went smoother thanks to Chris. The first week we did a few things together after school. One Monday we went to the library and started on a bio report. We were assigned to be partners for a paper on the effects of smoking. We headed to the library because it was quiet, and we found our own little corner in a secluded section. We always seemed to end up making out more than working on our report, though. "Chris, we shouldn't be doing this here."

"You know you don't want to stop," he said. "I can feel your want."

He was right. I didn't or couldn't stop. It got really heated; we were in one of the aisles looking for a book when all the sudden I was up against a shelf. Man, I thought we would do it in the library that day. The sprinklers could have gone off it was so hot. Our hands were all over each other. My hands wandered up his shirt feeling his soft skin against my fingers. I rubbed his chest and arms. All I could think about was how much I wanted him. The world felt shut out at the spark of all this. As his hands roamed my body, I was getting all hot and out of sorts. "Hmmm" I groan at his touch. "Don't stop, Chris. Please don't stop."

His hand found its way into the backside of my jeans softly squeezing my butt then moved around to the front to find my wetness. My fingers found their way to his hair and we kissed passionately as I tugged lightly. The sound of approaching voices snapped us back to reality. Quickly Chris pulled his hand from my pants, like a little kid caught with his hand in the cookie jar. An older woman walking past looked our way with a fake smile, as if she knew what we were doing.

"Hi!" Chris said, chuckling to the lady. He was standing in front of me with his hands on my thighs. I was resting my head on his back, while peeking subtly over his shoulder. As soon as she was out of sight, he turned around to me. "Amanda, you are so beautiful, I don't care if we got caught. Just feeling you is worth the risk." The sight of his hard on popping up his pants like a pitched tent made me laugh. He gave me a side glare and a snicker. I grabbed his hips and pulled him back to me.

"Hey, it's a good thing we were interrupted. Who knows what would have happened."

Looking down at me, he stared intently into my eyes. His hardness was pocking me in my belly and it made me laugh as it kind of tickled.

"You need to stop laughing, girl. It's not funny what you do to me. You see that hard on? Ya know I'll have the worst case of blue balls in history. If that lady didn't come, I'd be making you come right about now!"

"Oh yeah, you think so, cowboy? Who's to say it wouldn't be the other way around? That I wouldn't making you come?" I gave him another quick peck on the lips then I lightly tapped his cheek, turned and started back to our table. I needed to get out of there before our first time having sex was in the library.

We laughed our way back to our table and got our stuff together then headed out. Honestly, we waited a little longer before giving in, a few more days anyway. It was getting intense though, it was inevitable and soon.

We were very attracted to each other, but to keep us from rushing in to having sex. We did many other things though. Kept ourselves busy. We wanted nothing more than to keep things at a steady pace and to keep building on our feelings. Over the next several days we went to the batting cages, a park out of town, the mall, the movies, and played some pool, things that involved us not being alone.

We even went on a double date with Mark and his new girlfriend, Stacy. It seemed like this would be weird to Chris. His girlfriend's best friend being a guy. You know how insecure guys can be. He was a good sport, though, and was up for the double date. Chris and I have talked a lot about Mark's and mine close relationship, and I wanted to show Chris how much I adored my friendship with Mark. I also wanted to show Mark that I found happiness as well. It was good to be spending time with Mark again.

Mark and Stacy met us at a restaurant, a casual joint in downtown. There were booths and a few two-eater tables in the middle of the room. Stacy and Mark sat on one side, Chris, and I on the other. At first, I must admit it was a bit awkward. I didn't know Stacy and Mark didn't know Chris. Initially, it started out as quick introductions. Then Chris and I fell into our usual conversational sync. Thankfully, I noticed the silence across and beside me, and I changed the conversation to include Stacy and Mark. It wasn't intentional, it's just that when Chris and I were together, we finished each other's sentences.

After it turned into a group conversation, the night just seem to flow effortlessly. The four of us laughed a lot. Chris and Mark had a lot in common, and so did Stacy and me. She loved music as much as I did. All in all it was a blast. In fact, after that date, Chris told me that he and Mark wanted to hang out more. It went great.

**

Chris and I knew we weren't going to be able to hold out much longer. One Friday, after the last bell, I was standing at my locker when I felt lips on the back of my neck. It sent chills down my whole body. I closed my eyes and inhaled deep smelling his fresh cologne. I held my breath waiting for him to touch me again. He then put his mouth on my hot spot. His warm, moist tongue was on the back of my neck just behind my ear, first licking me then pressing his lips against me for a moment. Then nothing, but I could still feel his breath on my neck.

He put his strong arms around me then brought his mouth to my ear and I let out the breath I forgot I was holding and just melted. I could have been a puddle on the floor under his feet. The want and desire I had built up in my body was now an actual ache, my body hurt.

He whispered in my ear. "The way your ass looks in those jeans kills me. It actually made my heart skip when I was walking down the hallway and spotted you. I don't think I have ever wanted anything more than I want you. I can't hold it in anymore; I think I might actually combust into a million pieces."

I turned and kissed his lips, I couldn't hold it in anymore either. I had to have his lips on mine. "Chris, I don't think I can stand it much longer either. You make me want to do dirty things."

Just as I kissed him, we heard the sound of someone clearing their throat.

We stopped and slowly turned to find Mark standing there. "Hey love birds. Sorry to interrupt. I just wanted to let you know I'm having a party tomorrow night. My parents are going away."

"Hey Mark!" I kissed him on the cheek as I always do. "We'll try and stop by. I think we have a few things planned so we might not make it but we'll try." I turned and looked at Chris. "Right Chris?"

He smiled at me, knowing we didn't have plans but his parents were also going away for the weekend at a medical conference. "Yeah, sorry Mark. But I actually had some special plans for Amanda this weekend. We'll try though. Thanks for the invite."

I smiled at them and said to Mark, "If we don't make it, maybe sometime next week we can get together? Maybe another double date."

"That sounds good. Try to come though, it's gonna be a blast. Chris, take it easy on her, she's precious goods."

"Don't worry about that. I know what a rarity she is. We'll try to make it even if it's a short time."

I gave Mark another quick squeeze before grabbing Chris's hand, and pulling him toward the door. I yelled back to Mark, "I'll call you soon!"

When we got to the parking lot, Chris took me into his arms, gave me a passionate kiss, and, with his lips still on mine, said, "Meet me at my house."

We got in our cars and I followed him to his house.

I felt another surge of desire wash over me as I thought about being with Chris for the first time. I was getting nervous, yet I was excited. I really did want this to happen. I was sure we were ready. As I pulled up to Chris' house, I sat in my car listening to the rest of the song playing on the CD Chris had made for me. It reminded me of us. I thought about what it was going to be like to be with Chris and I was starting to get anxious.

I've heard stories from different girls in school. They talked about how guys were. They said how it happened so fast, there were no orgasms like what you read about in cosmopolitan. What they described sounded like it was only sex. Just sex and no love at all. I don't think it's gonna be like that with Chris and I. We do love each other. If I honestly thought it might or could be like that, I don't even think I would bother.

I started thinking, what if it hurt like last time. I know I shouldn't compare it to that, because that was one hundred percent different. I would be more relaxed now because I'd be wanting it this time. I wanted this and him. I loved him, and I knew for sure he felt the same.

I reached in my back seat and grabbed my overnight bag. Clean clothes, underwear, bra, bathing suit, makeup, deodorant, a razor, and perfume. It really had everything and anything that I could possibly need, except condoms. I hoped he had condoms.

Walking up to the front door, my heart was pounding. I'm going to have a heart attack.I can literally see my heart pounding in my chest. I knocked at the door and heard him yell, "Come in, it's open."

I opened the door. I still can't get over his house and how beautiful it was. It looked like it's straight out of a Good Housekeeping magazine or something. Everything looked expensive and elegant; his mom had great but simple taste.

I heard music coming from his room. As I started walking up the stairs, I could hear him singing. I realized I had never heard him sing before and I was shocked at what an amazing voice he had. It made me beyond happy. I loved music, I loved him, and he could sing--a dream come true.

His room smelled of vanilla. There must have been about 20 candles burning. He was sitting on the edge of his bed, taking off his sneakers. He then stood up and pulled down his pants.

"Wow, eager cowboy?"

"If you don't mind Amanda, I was gonna hop in the shower. I had gym today."

I started feeling very embarrassed and humiliated.

"Sorry. Go take a shower. I'll wait here."

He flashed me a sexy smile. "I am very eager though, just so you know."

I would have given anything to have my own bathroom.

I dropped my bag on the floor and looked around his room. Over his computer desk was a large cork board, and pinned to it were cards, notes, papers, and pictures. There was a bunch of pictures of us, actually. They were all snapshots of me laughing or smiling. I hadn't even seen some of them yet.

There was the one he took at the restaurant. Our heads were cut off a little but the smiles on our faces were that of pure happiness. I spotted a couple of me alone that he must have taken when I wasn't looking. Then there was one of me from the Red Sox game, and another from when we went to the batting cages. There was one of me laughing from last week at a park out of town. I didn't even realize he had a camera that day--or most of those days, actually.

He started singing again from the shower and the idea to join him just came to me. I started undressing quickly and headed to the door. I put my hand on the handle, turned it, and took a deep breath.

As the door opened, he immediately stopped singing. He wiped the glass and peered at me, naked as I was walking his way. My heart was pounding practically out of my chest.

He slid open the door and all I could see was his beautiful dripping wet body. "You are amazing Christopher."

"You just stole that word right from my mouth. Sorry I didn't speak sooner, but you took my breath away."

I smiled, stepped into the shower, and immediately our mouths were touching. At that instant, all the nervousness I had vanished. I knew at that moment that this was right. Our lips pressed hard against each other, tongues twisting and twirling around each other's. Our hands were all over each other touching, groping, and needing. The feeling I had at this moment was something I never thought I would ever have. I felt complete. Being with Chris was amazing no matter what. I felt desire, want, need, happiness, and above all, security.

We started slowing down and came to a slow kiss then we stopped. He kept his lips on mine and said, "My god, Amanda, you are so beautiful. Your body is perfect. I never thought it could look this good. I've imagined it so many times, but never this good. I feel so much desire for you. You truly are perfect, and beautiful. I love you!"

He could always do that to me, say all the right things and make my heart melt. "I love you, too, Chris."

He grabbed the soap, a washcloth, and started washing my body. He told me to turn around, and I did happily. He gently, but slowly washed my back, arms, butt, thighs, legs, and feet. He moved in front of me then he started on the front side of me. He took the time and washed all of me. He put the cloth down then pulled me under the water. Now he was slowly rubbing his hands all over my body, helping the water rinse the suds off me.

"Amanda, you are so beautiful, there's nowhere else I'd rather be then here with you. Now, I'm going to get to know every part of your body. I know your heart is made of gold and your mind is adventurous, but your body, I want to know every crevasse." All I could think about was how truly amazing he is. He is patient, sensual, caring, thoughtful, kind, loving, and sincere.

"I want you to feel every part of me. I want to get to know your body too. I want you so much."

After speaking those words, he shut off the water and stepped out. He grabbed a towel, and proceeded to dry every square inch of my body just as gentle as he washed me.

Then he led me to his bedroom. He brushed my long blonde hair as he spoke to me.

"I've thought about this night for a long time. I don't want to rush you or make you feel that you have to do something you don't want or aren't ready for."

"I'm here with you and I'm more than ready. There's no place I'd rather be right now than with you. I want to make love to you, here and now."

He took me by the hand and led me to his bed. "Hmm then show me."

He took off my towel and threw it over a chair. He stood there looking at me, at my body, not touching yet. I did the same to him; I was taking it all in. Completely connecting to this moment and what was about to happen. I stood there soaking in the guy I was ready to willingly give myself to and my heart warmed. I knew with all my heart that I was truly ready for this, for him.

"Are you sure you want this, Amanda? I don't want you to feel any pressure."

"I'm one hundred percent sure. I promise you that."

"I've never wanted anything more than I want you right now. Come over here so I can taste those lips."

I lay down on his bed and he crawled up to kiss me. As his lips brushed mine, my whole body relaxed. I felt so warm, my body aching with desire. His mouth started trailing down my neck.

"I am going to kiss, and touch, every part of your body."

"I think that I'm going to like that very much," I told him.

He was now at my chest when his mouth found my breast. My nipple was in his mouth and I got really hot and tingly. The area between my thighs was pulsating. I knew from just that feeling alone that I will be feeling many new feelings tonight.

As he sucked on my nipples, I needed to touch him. I ran my fingers through his thick dark blonde hair. I then went to his neck then down his back, and then I grabbed his ass. That hard ass pushed me over the edge. I wanted him more than I could have ever imagined.

Completely distracted with the way I was feeling, I didn't even notice he was already at my waist, just about to my wetness. His mouth felt right on my body. My belly had butterflies as his hot breath fell on me, sending chills down my whole body.

He looked up at me and smiled that sexy smile, the one that melts me inside. I smiled back and he put his mouth on me, his mouth was on my...

I stopped myself from thinking. Holy hell, it felt so good. My hips lifted off the bed.

"Ahhh, Chris, what are you doing?" He stopped and looked up.

"Does that hurt?"

I couldn't breathe. I couldn't speak or move. I was frozen.

"Do you want me to stop?"

"I, no, I... Oh my god what was that? That felt amazing, No don't stop, please."

He laughed.

"I thought that it hurt. I want to keep licking and tasting you if it feels good."

"Oh my god yes please. That felt absolutely amazing. I never felt anything like that before. Remember, tonight is all new to me."

He stopped again and began to speak but I stopped him. "No, no, no, please don't talk, keep doing that."

He chuckled into me. Oh the vibration,it sent a shock through my body, right to my core. It was defiantly something different I was experiencing at this moment. He kept his tongue in action for a few minutes, and then I completely lost it when he put his finger inside me.

"You are getting so wet. You like this don't you?"

I had no idea this would feel so good.

"Yes, I like it, yes!"

I couldn't take it anymore. I wanted to kiss him, touch him, and make him feel this good.

Then it hit me. A wave of pure ecstasy went through my body like a jolt. My body felt shaky, I was pulsating inside, and my legs were beginning to shake. This was by far the most stimulating yet most amazing feeling I have ever had. I couldn't take it anymore. I needed his mouth on mine. I didn't even care where his mouth just was. I wanted him and I wanted him now.

"Wow that was awesome. That felt amazing. Where did you learn that?"

"Porn. My brother left it for me when he left for college."

"Well, thank him for me!"

I then started kissing him and doing for him what he did to me. I worked my way down the hardness of his body. Tenderly kissing and licking his pecks, stomach, then I got to his package. All I thought to myself was that dicks were somewhat ugly, but his was nice. Not like the pictures we saw in health class.

I took him in my hand and slid it up and down his length a few times. Watching his face in the process, I was trying to tell if it felt good. Judging from the low groans coming from his mouth it must have felt good. I was watching my hand move up and down him, and I couldn't help but think that this was going to be inside me. It was so large. Much bigger than I expected.

I then put my head down toward him, opened my mouth, relaxed, and put it over him. Filling my mouth with him, he moaned loudly. I started bobbing my head up and down his length as I did with my hand, knowing he liked that. As I was doing this, I started sucking lightly, almost like I was drinking from a giant straw. I thought he liked what I was doing, but then he stopped me; put his hands on my head.

"Honey, stop please. Come here and kiss me. If you keep that up, I will cum before we get to make love."

I crawled back up to him and put my mouth over his kissing him with all I had. I wanted him inside me now the anticipation was killing me.

"Do you have a condom?"

"Of course I do." I got them last week after our session at the library."

He got up off the bed and walked over to his dresser. Opening the top draw, he pulled out a dark blue box of condoms. He took two out and walked back to the bed. The whole time I was watching him intently, checking out his fine body. He was so handsome and so happy. He had a smile from ear to ear.

He got back to the bed and sat on the edge. I sat up and put my chin on his shoulder. "You okay, Chris?"

"Yeah I'm more than okay. I just don't want to rush this. I want to be with you more than I ever thought possible but I don't want anything to change between us."

I couldn't believe that he was the one thinking these things. Was he real? I pinched him on the back of the arm.

"Ouch, what was that for?"

"I was just checking to make sure that you were real. I love you so much, and believe me when I say that I don't think things will change. I want to be with you more than I ever thought would be possible for me. There are always things that change but we aren't one of those things. I think we'll be together for a long time. Unless you realize that you want someone better, someone prettier, or something."

He turned his head fast and grabbed both sides of my head.

"No, no, I only want you, no one else. I would be fine if we didn't have sex. Just being with you is enough for me."

I loved that he was so genuine with me. So I needed to bust his balls. To lighten him up. I started to get off the bed and walked toward the pile of clothes I left on the floor.

"Hot damn, I'm a lucky guy!"

"Hey, wait, where are you going? What are you doing?"

"Hey you said you were fine with not having sex, I'm getting dressed." I bent over to pick up my shirt

"Oh no you don't! There's no way I'm letting you get away."

He got up, quickly and ran over to me. He was so fast almost tripping, but he stopped, froze, completely still. I looked back over my shoulder, and realized it was because I was completely naked and I was bent over.

I started laughing and said, "Stare much?

He was still in shock, I think at the site of my ass in the air. I saw him start to move when I stood up quick, and ran.

I jumped on his bed and screamed. He jumped up on the bed and grabbed me. Then I attacked him.

We started going at it hard. He put his foot behind mine, with one of his hands on my back and one on the back of my head. He then pushed his foot back sweeping me off my feet. I landed on my back, with him now straddling above me. My body was responding to his.

I pulled up and started kissing him again. He moved his hips ever so slightly and his dick brushed against my upper thigh. All I felt was wet. He was starting to leak. I looked down and grabbed it, I started stroking him, he bent down and put his mouth on my tit, pulling on my nipple with his teeth and I was done.

"Chris, I need you now! I can't wait anymore."

"That's good because I could finish just looking at you."

He sat up, reached over to where he must have dropped the condom, ripped it open, and started rolling it down over himself.

I was filled to the brink with desire. He was now above me, ready to fill me, when he paused; he was looking into my eyes, searching them to make sure this is what I really wanted.

"I love you. Please, I need this more than you know."

He lowered himself to my opening and gently pushed forward. I held my breath for a moment then let it out when he was about half way in. I was happy he was going very slow, only putting a little at a time. I kept my eyes on his and my hands on his shoulders. He continued to push slowly until he was all the way in. He then paused for a minute, I think for me to adjust to him. He bent down and kissed me, he was shaking, and so was I. He took his mouth and gazed.

"I can't believe this is real. I've wanted you for so long and now I have you. This is right we belong together. I love you so much, Amanda."

A tear ran down my face; I wasn't hurt or in pain, I was truly and utterly happy. The tears started flowing. "I love you, too. More than you know."

He then started moving his hips slowly. I closed my eyes, at that very moment all I wanted to do was just only feel, not see. I wanted to feel what it was like to be loved and to make love. I wanted to feel this, what I was experiencing. I wanted this to erase the only other memory I had seared in my brain. This had to replace that. He was going in and out as slow as he could. I could tell he was holding back. I opened my eyes and looked up at his face. He also had a tear rolling down his cheek. The look I saw in his eyes was that of complete happiness and love. I hope that's what he saw in mine to because that's all there is now. No more fear or pain. Now all I have is love, desire, and happiness. We continued on slow and steady, until we both climaxed. We lay together still connected and we both said at the same time, "I love you!"

We stayed up for a long time after that just talking. We talked about everything imaginable. We were wrapped up in a blanket and each other. It felt so good to be with him, to be held by him, and to be loved by him. I was so happy in that time. I never really thought that I could feel like this. He was holding me so that with one hand he was running his finger through my hair and with the other he was running up, and down my back. I felt safe, light, comfort, peace, and extreme happiness. I remember starting to drift off and trying so hard to stay awake. I just couldn't resist so I gave in to sleep. We woke the next morning still holding each other. I don't even think we moved all during the night.

It was wonderful waking up with him. I decided to give him a little wake up tease. Well it couldn't be just a tease I guess. Because we gave in to desire and made love once more. It was incredible. We then showered and hung around his house all day. We were taking full advantage of his parents not being home. We ordered pizza for lunch and watched movies. It was such a perfect day. I couldn't have asked for a better first and second time. We definitely were happy and in love, there was   no   doubt   about   that.

Ann's Home

The weeks passed slowly after Chris and I had made love. We had had sex a couple of times since that night, both times being equally as good or better. It was extremely hard to fight the urge to be together. However, when it did happen things moved slowly no rushing. It was just taking the time to show each other our feelings for one another.

Every day spent together made our connection and relationship so much stronger. He remembered every little thing I said. He noticed the little things, where someone else may not have noticed. We talked about everything, getting closer and closer to one another's souls. The way he looked at me made me feel like I was the only girl in the world.

When Ann came back from her trip, and I knew she wanted my full attention again. She loved her trip and her excitement made me want to travel the world and see other cultures. I could picture

Chris and I traveling together and making love in other countries. The thought made me so happy and horny.

Ann and I missed each other so much. The day she came back was a Friday afternoon; she was tired from the time change and the traveling. I slept over Friday and Saturday. It rained all day so we just hung inside. We watched Friends on DVD all day and night. We could always do just the simplest things. It may have seemed boring to others, but we truly loved spending time together even if it was doing nothing. We talked all night long about everything that has happened since she was gone.

"So, we made love. Ann, it was incredible, I'm so in love with him."

"Oh my god, you did? Did it hurt?"

"He was incredible. The first time he was so gentle. It was beautiful. I never thought it would be like that."

"I've been thinking it may be time for Jason and me to take that next step too. What do you think?"

"I think that you shouldn't do it because you feel pressured to, you should only do it if you feel ready and that it's right. At first I was nervous with just the thought of it but then I knew, he was the right one for me."

"Jason doesn't put any pressure on me. He's been great and I do think I'm finally ready."

One Sunday afternoon, Ann and I headed to the pharmacy and picked up some condoms, just in case, along with a few other necessities. Then we went to lunch. We called the boys to meet us but they were both unavailable. Jason was at his grandparents for their traditional family Sunday dinner, while Chris was home sick in bed. He thought he had a stomach bug or something.

We ate lunch and I went to Chris's house while Ann went home. I felt bad for him stuck in bed all day.

"I brought you some soup and ice cream to help you feel better," I told him.

"Thanks, hon. Just seeing you I feel better already."

"Can I get you anything, do you want some soup?"

"Not yet, thanks. Can you lay down with me and we can watch a movie?"

"I'd love to, I want you to feel all better."

We lay on his bed and watched a movie and we both fell asleep. When I woke up, I watched him sleep for a bit until he began to stir. He needed to eat something; he had to build up his strength. I went down in the kitchen and heated up some soup for him. When I got back with the soup and crackers, he was throwing up in his trash barrel.

"Are you okay?"

"I'll be fine once I get this out."

I got behind him on the bed carefully not to make the bed shake and I rubbed his back.

"Amanda, honey. I love that you're here, but I don't want to get you sick."

"Don't you worry that handsome head of yours."

I didn't want to leave him, but I also didn't want to get sick. I was torn between whether to stay or go. Then I realized I couldn't leave him. His parents were out; he needed someone to take care of him. So I stayed in with him and took care of him for the rest of the night.

His parents arrived home about ten o'clock.

"Hi, sorry I'm here so late," I told them, "but Chris has been sick all day. I didn't feel comfortable leaving him."

"Thank you for taking care of him, Amanda. I'm sorry we weren't here."

"I brought him some soup and ice cream. He tried a little of the soup, but he threw it up. I have been squirting water in his mouth so at least he has some fluids."

"You're a good little nurse, Amanda. We're glad you are here."

"I'm going to go check on him and head home. He needs rest."

I went up to his room and he was sound asleep. I didn't want to wake him, so I left him a note on his desk.

Dear Chris,

I hope you feel better soon. Call me if you need anything at all, even if you just want to say hi. Make sure you keep drinking fluids and get plenty of rest. I need my man to be healthy.

I love you,

Amanda

I kissed him on the forehead, told him I loved him, and then went home.

Chris wasn't in school the next day. I called and checked on him during lunch and he was still feeling the same. Chris and I got an A on our bio report. I was so excited I couldn't wait to tell him. At the end of the day before, going over to check on Chris, I decided to go to the store and get him a little get well gift.

I walked around the store, looking at everything trying to decide what to get him. I saw a cute little stuffed animal I thought would be perfect for him, just like Chris a gorilla is smart, strong, loyal, but can be very loving and cuddly.

I drove to his house and knocked on the door. His mother answered the door and welcomed me in.

"Hi, Mrs. Jenkins. How's the patient today?"

"He was up most of the night but he's finally sleeping."

"Oh, poor guy. I was hoping he would be feeling better today. I don't want to bother him but I picked him up something small."

"That's so sweet. You can go on up and see if he's awake."

When I got to Chris's room, he was still sleeping. He looked peaceful and that made me feel better. He needs his rest to get better. I didn't want to wake him so I left him another note.

Dear Chris,

I came by to give you a get well present. It's nothing big, but it reminded me of you. I miss you. I hate that you're still sick. Cuddle up with the gorilla and he'll make you feel better. Gorilla's are smart, caring, and strong and loving, just like you. Get better!

I love everything about you my little gorilla.

Amanda

***

Several days went by, and he was still feeling the same. He stopped throwing up but still felt crappy. He came back to school and was just pushing through the days. It sucked because the next several weeks were going to be very busy. The next few weekends I had several trips with my mom, Ann, and Holly lined up to visit colleges.

Chris and I were talking and spending as much time together as possible, but getting things ready and planned was taking up a lot of time. We also were now in mid-term study mode, along with planning for Christmas.

Mine and Ann's first choice of school was Boston University. Chris came along with us to check it out, and I knew BU was where I belonged.

A week before Christmas, Ann and I went shopping for the guys. Along the way, Ann had stopped and picked up some new underwear and a bra as she was planning their special night. I bought a few new things for myself as well, thinking it had been about two weeks since Chris and I had made love. He still wasn't feeling like himself.

I was excited to shop for our very first Christmas together. I got him a new iPod, and downloaded tons of music onto it. I was sure this Christmas would be the first of many, for us, and I knew he felt the same way.

My mom was noticing how different I have been since being with Chris. She was over the moon happy for me.

"Amanda, I know you love Chris and he you, but I just want you two to enjoy this and not rush it. You two are still young and have plenty of time."

"Mom, I know. We are not rushing into getting married or anything. We're just in love."

"You'd have to be blind to not see that sparkle in your eye. The love is showing all over your face. Just take it slow."

"Will do, Mom!"

I was very excited that I was going to be introducing Chris to my Dad, Grandma, and Grandpa at Christmas. I couldn't wait for them to finally meet the boy who had stolen my heart four months before.

The following day I was at Chris's house. His parents were at work. We were up in his room.

"Let me help you clean up this mess," I told him. "It will impress your mother."

"She'll know that you helped me. I've never been good at cleaning."

"I'm so excited for Christmas and you meeting my family. They are going to love you like I do."

"I hope they do. I'm looking forward to meeting them, too. I thought I would be nervous but I'm not."

"No need to be nervous. They will love you!"

He finished putting his clothes away and I laid on his bed. He looked at me with a devious smile and jumped on the bed to join me. I was laughing at him and he started tickling me.

"I really love to hear you laugh Amanda! So I'm going to keep tickling you."

I was laughing so hard, he seemed to know exactly all the right places that tickled the most.

"You... need to... stop! Chris...I'm gonna pee...your bed!"

He then abruptly stopped and continued to laugh.

"No please don't do that. I have to sleep here."

I got up.

"I think you stopped just in time!. Gotta go now!"

Walking to the bathroom, I looked back at him. He was lying propped up on one arm with his hand in his hair. Damn he looked so sexy. I quickly went to the bathroom. As I stood at the sink washing, my hands I couldn't help but feel that need for him. I dried my hands then checked myself in the mirror, fixing my hair that was just messed up from his little tickle session. I think I want to surprise him.

Chris was still in the same position on the bed, still staring at the bathroom. I gave him a sexy smirk, to which he raised his eyebrow in curiosity. I started slowly walking towards him. As I did, I grabbed the bottom of my shirt and pulled it over my head, tossing it on the floor. I then stopped to undo my jeans, and pulled them down slowly as I stepped out of them. I reached behind my back, unclasping my bra. I took down each strap, pausing as I did. Then I tossed the bra at him. I took couple more steps and stopped right before the bed. I was amazed at how this whole time he stayed focused on me. I then put my hands on either side of my lace thong and started to slowly pull them down my thighs slowly. I stepped out of them and knelt on the bed.

He smiled a Cheshire cat grin as I walked on my knees to him, pulling one leg over him, so that I was straddling him. I bent down and kissed him with tenderness. I then pulled him to sit up and I take off his shirt. I pushed him back down to the bed, taking myself off of him to undo his pants and toss them on the floor. With a little exciting tease I peeled down his boxer briefs. His hardness sprung out and I got back on top of him.

Kissing his lips lightly and then working my way down his body took his hardness in my hand. I licked the tip and worked my tongue over it, wrapping my lips over him. I kept up my pace for a while, enjoying pleasuring him and the noises he makes, and the expressions on his face.

Trying to warn me that he was getting close, he wanted me to stop but I wasn't having it. He has pleasured me before while letting me cum. I only want to do the same for him. I then felt him tense beneath me. He put his hands on my shoulders then released himself into my mouth. I continued on slowly moving until he was done.

Pulling me up to him, he gave me a light peck me on the lips. I laughed, but I understood.

"That was amazing, Amanda!"

I told him that I was happy to do it. I liked making him feel good.

We were pulled out of our moment when we heard the front door shut so we quickly got up gathering our clothes. I swiped mine up fast and ran back into the bathroom. When I got in there I realized I had no bra. I just started laughing to myself while getting the rest of my clothes on. It didn't really matter because I knew that his parents wouldn't come up here if they saw my car. They had been good about not coming to his room when I was there. I went back into his room and he was all dressed and sitting on the edge of his bed. He was playing his guitar so I just stood there for a minute watching him. Then he started to sing. At that moment as he sang, I had no word to describe my feelings. I was just simply happy and in love.

On the Sick List

We were at my house on Christmas Eve for an early family dinner. My sister, Samantha, was down for family time and our gift exchange. She brought her new beau with her, Chase. They had been dating for a year now I couldn't wait to introduce her to Chris. We invited Chris's parents but they were going in to work for a little while to help out, as the holidays tended to get busy. They had told me that since Chris was older now they liked to spend the day with family and the nights taking care of others' loved ones.

My mom and I cooked a nice roast beef dinner with mashed potatoes, gravy, carrots, corn, bread, salad, apple pie, and caramel brownies. When I opened the door, I lost my breath for a minute ,seeing my handsome love standing there, all cute, with a bouquet of flowers.

"These are for your mom," he said. He came in and I happily introduced him to my sister and, Chase. I walked over to my mom in the kitchen, gave her the flowers, and told her that Chris brought them for her.

As my mom was admiring and smelling the flowers, I grabbed a vase to put them in. Chris walked in.

"Hi Laura you look lovely today." He gave her a kiss on the cheek. I thought that was so nice.

My mom laughingly told him, "Ya okay! You are such a suck up." She shook her head in disbelief.

"No, really you do. You are glowing with happiness."

"If anyone's glowing with happiness, it's Amanda you guys. You are so in love. You're young but you can see it's not just that teenage crush with you love birds." Shaking her head she then returned a kiss to his cheek. "Thank you for making my daughter happy. I've never seen Amanda so happy and laugh as much, probably since she was a baby.

He blushed instantly. "I love Amanda so much, and I know I will forever. I don't care how young I am."

"Forever Chris?" I couldn't believe my ears. Chris will love me forever. Best present ever.

"Yes, I think so!" He gave me the sweetest loving smile and I knew he meant it.

This sense of peace washed over me after hearing this. My sister walked in asking if she could set the table, my mom handed her a stack of plates and I went over to grab the silverware leaving my mom and Chris to talk. In the dining room, my sister and I set the table. As I help set the table I couldn't help think about what Chris had just said to my mom. I wonder what they are talking about at that moment.

"Hey, you over there, all smiles. What's up? What are you thinking about? Chris?"

"Yeah, he's all I think about when I'm not with him," I said, smiling ear to ear. I looked up to try and read her face.

"Ummm you know he's only in the other room right?"

"Ahh, yeah, dur! I was just thinking about a conversation I had with mom this morning. She told me that she thought Chris was a cutie. Along with mentioning her concerns about us being young but seeing us together she just knew, it made her happier just to see me happy. She also said something along the lines of, 'I don't want to hold you back from happiness. You've been kept from that for too long. I trust you to be safe and make the right decisions.' It made me even more happy knowing how she felt. It means a lot to me to have her support. Cause in my heart I know that Chris is the right choice for me. He's such a great guy."

"Well, as long as you use your brains and be smart. That's all I can say. I don't want you to be my first patient," she said with a snicker.

"I am safe so you don't have to worry," I said.

Shortly after setting the table we were ready to eat, we sat down and ate a delicious dinner together. Chris really wasn't eating that much.

"Hey, Honey, if you don't like the food, it was all my sister she cooked it." I kept my head down as I played with my food acting casual as I knew she'd be giving me an evil eye.

"No no, it's good. Really. I ate a huge lunch," he said. "Plus, I want to save room for dessert."

After dinner, Chris and I sat in my room and listened to music. We started talking about the day we had planned for tomorrow. Then I noticed that he seemed to lose his balance when he tried to stand up, and quickly sat down on my bed. He looked rather pale. I rushed over to him.

"Are you okay?" Suddenly feeling a little panicked. He looked like he was going to pass out.

"Yeah I'm okay. I think I just stood up too fast."

I told him that I was going to go grab him a glass of water and to lie down. I went into the kitchen and told Samantha what had happened and she said she was gonna go check him out. As I was getting him some water, my mom had come into the kitchen with a few bags from the store. She saw my concern and I told her what happened.

She said the same thing as Samantha; she wanted to check him out.

We walked into my room, he was lying on my bed, and my sister was checking his pulse. My mom asked him how he felt and he said a bit dizzy, she went into the other room and grabbed her bag; she came back in and took his blood pressure.

I knew my sister and mom were talking about him and I was dying not knowing what was going on. The look on their faces was making me even more nervous as they looked confusingly at each other.

"He has low blood pressure and a weak pulse. Maybe you should call his parents."

I called his mom. "Cara, I think Chris is sick. Something is wrong."

"What's wrong, sweetie?"

I told her what Samantha and my mom had said. I also said that I was really worried about him. She said she was on a shift at the hospital and asked if I could drive him and meet her at the hospital ER. Chase and my mom helped him to the car. My sister was gonna stay back and finish cleaning up. I think she saw the panic in my face and whispered to me that she wasn't a doctor yet but she believed he would be fine. Maybe he just had a virus or something.

My mom drove while Chris and I sat in the back seat together. I told him how much I loved him

"I love you too. I am so sorry for ruining your Christmas with all this."

"You didn't ruin my Christmas at all. Don't ever think that. You already made it the best ever, plus you are my life whether you like it or not and I'm staying right by your side."

He leaned into me while resting his head on my shoulder.

When we arrived at the ER, Cara was waiting outside with a wheelchair. When Chris spotted her he instantly lifted his head from my shoulder sitting straight up. "I don't need a wheelchair, I'm not handicapped."

My mom tilted her head and looked slightly over her shoulder. "Oh, Chris, you're weak honey . Just use it. Amanda, I'll back when you need a ride home. I hope you feel better Chris!"

We helped him out of the car and into the chair; Cara bent down and kissed his head. "Where's Dad?

"He's in the middle of surgery. He'll be here as soon as he can. He had a call sent down to the ER doctor. He'll report to him and keep him updated. He said he loves you." I wheeled him into the hospital where Cara finished checked him in at the ER registration.

The nurse came out to get Chris; I was going to stay behind and wait in the waiting area. As I was watching, the nurse and Cara walk and talk, while pushing the wheelchair down the hall, all I was thinking about was my love is sick. Then all of the sudden they stopped walking and Cara called down the hall.

"Amanda, sweetheart, can you please come here a minute?"

I got up and walked over to them. Chris turned to me and said, "When I am all set in the room, will you come in and sit with me?"

"Of course I will. I am here for you, I'm not going anywhere."

I wanted to spend Christmas with my family but at the same time I wanted nothing more than to not leave his side.

He smiled wide. It was a joy to see.

"Okay then I will see you soon. Love you!"

As they headed away, I called out "I love you, too, my little Gorilla." Then all I heard was him laughing.

His mom looked back, smiled and gave me a wink. I smiled back at her and sat down in the waiting area for what seemed like an eternity.

After the longest hour and fifteen minutes of my life, Cara came out and said the doctor was just finishing up with check him out, they ran a few simple test and they said he has a virus and is severely dehydrated. They are giving him some medicine and fluids thru the IV and he has to stay overnight tonight to be monitored because he has low blood pressure. A wash of relief came over me as I felt he would be okay. Cara said she was going back to their house to grab a few things and that she'd be back in a little bit. She told me to go down to his room; she said he was very tired but anxiously awaiting me to come.

I walked down the hall and got to his room. I found myself standing outside the door, not realizing that I was barely breathing and I had to catch my breath. I was having a panic attack. I tried to think about what Dr. Baker would tell me to do. It had been such a long time since I had a panic attack.

I took five deep breaths and released them, and I felt a bit better. Just as I was to open his door, I heard, "Ah, you must be Amanda. I just heard so much about you."

I was a little surprised and still coming out of my calming zone so I stumbled on my words, "Um, I oh, I, yes, yes. I am sorry."

"Chris was just talking about how he was waiting patiently for his angel to come see him."

I smiled politely. "He was talking about me?"

He smiled and said, "Yes I am sure it is you. You are just as beautiful as he described, so it has to be you. Amanda right?"

I blushed. "Yes, I am Amanda, Chris's girlfriend." I reached out my hand to him.

He took it, shook firmly.

"I'm Dr. Brown. I'm the attending on tonight. Our patient is resting, but please go in so he can rest better knowing you're here. He should be headed up to a real room soon. It was a pleasure meeting you." I put a smile on my face while trying to hide my nerves and went into Chris's room. I saw him lying in the bed with his head turned and eyes closed. I quietly walked over and sat in the chair next to his bed not wanting to wake him. Watching him sleep was always so peaceful to me. I'd had the chance to watch him a lot over the past month, since he first got sick, he'd been napping a lot. He started to wake up.

"Hey beautiful."

I gave him the biggest smile, got up, and kissed his cheek.

"Hey, handsome. How are you feeling?"

I placed my hand on his arm to just touch him enough to let him know that I was really there for him.

He waited a moment before answering me and said, "I feel really tired and weak."

I gave him a frown. "Maybe once you get some of that medicine and fluids into you, you'll feel better."

"Yeah maybe you are right. Hey where's my mom?"

"She went to your house to grab a few things."

"Maybe you can call her and ask her to bring my gorilla?"

I smiled at the thought that he wanted to have it with him.

We sat silently just looking at each other. He gave me that sexy smirk that just melts my heart. A feeling of sadness washed over me and a tear ran down my cheek. I felt so helpless, just knowing that there was nothing I could say, nor do that would make him feel better.

"Honey, what's wrong? Why are you crying?"

I kept looking at him, never taking my eyes off his. It was like I was trying to read his mind. He said again, "What?" As he reached out his hand to me and said, "Amanda love, please don't cry. I don't want to see you sad. I'm fine, I will be fine."

"You most certainly will be."

I turned to see Cara standing there. I quickly wiped my face, feeling silly for crying when she was so peppy. She was back from the house. She was carrying one of his backpacks and the gorilla.

"Mom you brought my gorilla, I was gonna call you and ask you to bring it for me."

"Well I figured you'd want it since you've slept with it every night since Amanda gave it to you."

We all started laughing and he said, "Hey don't say that too loud."

We just kept laughing, for me because I thought it so cute that he slept with every night and his mom, because he was eighteen years old and sleeping with a stuffed animal.

As we sat in the room talking, a nurse came in and said she was going to be taking Chris up to a real room. She adjusted his cords and started unlocking the wheels on the bed.

"I guess I'm moving on up. I will see you beautiful ladies soon."

"You most certainly are."

I started gathering his things while Cara signed some papers at the registration desk. I looked around the room and made sure I had everything and I saw his wallet on the counter by sink, I walked over and picked it up, taking a glance inside just to make sure it was his. Inside I saw his license so I knew it was. I went to close it back up when Cara walked back in. "You all set? Cone on we can walk up to his room together."

That's when a picture had fallen out of his wallet. I bent down and picked it up. It was our first picture we took together at that restaurant in Boston, the day of the Red Sox game. I went to put it back inside the wallet when I noticed the writing on the back: "The love of my life, the day I fell in love." Tears started falling from my eyes.

"Amanda honey, what's wrong?" I looked up at her with the tears now flowing like a river.

"This picture fell out of Chris's wallet. It's from our first real date."

"Amanda he is going to be okay."

"No Cara, it's not that. It's what he wrote on the back.

She took it from my hand and read it.

"That's so sweet, he is so sweet. You know he loves you so much. He's always talking about you. I don't think I have ever seen him so happy in his life. Even when he was a baby he wasn't happy. When we adopted him he wasn't happy. He was happy as a kid though. I think probably around the time of middle school. That is when he first saw you, in sixth grade. I remember the day he came home from school and he told us, 'Mom...Dad I met the love of my life today in the library at school. She is beautiful and her name is Amanda Nelson. He's truly never been as happy since he started dating you."

While I was happy yo hear he talked about me all the time, I was a little shocked finding out he was adopted. He never told me. He looked like his parents. I was so confused.

"I'm sorry, but I have to ask... Chris has never told me that he was adopted. Does he know?"

"Yes, he knows but he doesn't talk about it, not even to us. We told him when he was young because he doesn't remember much. His biological dad, Andrew, and Spencer were brothers. His biological mother, Karen, and I were best friends. They died in a car accident when he was just, ten months old. Chris was in the car when it happened, but miraculously he didn't get hurt. Not even one scratch on him. Back when it happened, I used to work as a nurse in the ER and

Spencer was working as a doctor there as well. We were both on duty the night of the accident. When they brought them into the ER, I recognized the crying first."

Cara seemed so lost while she was telling me all this. Sucked back into the horrible time, lost in the memory and pain she felt.

"I was sitting at the nurse's station making notes in a chart that was when I heard the doors opened and I heard Chris's cry. I babysat him a lot when he was a baby. Plus Karen and I spent a lot of time together. I looked up and saw two stretchers with them on it and an EMT was holding Chris. My heart dropped to my feet, I could barely stand knowing this is my best friend, her sweet baby, and my brother in law. I pushed through that night and helped all I could to save them. Andrew died pretty much on impact and Karen survived until the following night. She ended up having a few surgeries fixing several of the traumas; she was a brave and very strong woman. We thought she was going to pull through. She had woken up the morning after the accident. Spencer and I had slept at the hospital that night with Chris. I thought it could give her some strength. When she woke up she asked to hold him, she told us to take care of him, to love him as our own. I knew at that moment that she knew she wasn't going to make it. I told her that I loved her and I would do anything for her. I did and always would love Chris as my own. Spencer told her the same thing. He was one of the greatest gifts to me. After having Ryan, the doctors had to do an emergency hysterectomy because I was hemorrhaging. So we then could no longer have any more kids. We both wanted a few more so we planned to adopt anyway. Well, we can talk about this anytime but I think we should get back up to Chris."

I was crying hysterically at that point, knowing that Chris too had been carrying his own painful secret, that he had never known his real parents.

She gave me a big bear hug and said, "I am thankful for you being here as I know it means a lot to my boy. I know he loves you and you love him. I am truly happy you two are together." She then gave me a kiss on the cheek. "Now let's get going and see our boy," she said.

I looked at her smiled. "Thank you for sharing that story with me. I know it must have been hard for you. I want you to know that I love Chris with all my heart and will forever, and always."

Bittersweet

Well, Christmas Eve hadn't turned out like any of us had planned. It's times like these that you really sit back and realize what's important. I love Christmas and yes, I was so looking forward to sharing it with Chris. I will be sharing is with Chris, just not in the way we had planned, but ya know, I would not have it any other way. I wasn't leaving him to be alone on Christmas Eve.

Spencer talked with Chris and Chris didn't want me to leave either. Lucky for us, he had strings he could pull at the hospital so I was able to stay.

"Dr. Jenkins, thank you so much for allowing me to stay the night with Chris."

"He's going to be just fine and he would much rather have you here than his parents. Call us if you need anything at all."

"I will, Merry Christmas."

I ended up spending the night at the hospital with Chris; sleeping on a very uncomfortable pink pull-out chair bed contraption.

Sometime during the night, Chris's IV monitor went off and it woke me up. When the nurse was in the room changing the IV bag I asked her if she thought if it would be okay if I lay on the bed with him. She said yes which made me happy because even though he was asleep I just wanted to comfort him.

I had climbed in on the side with no IV, and snuggled in under his arm. I hadn't slept in the same bed as Chris since the weekend we first made love. I feel at ease when I'm with him. He was the sick one yet he still made me safe and so loved. I think he liked it too because even though he was out like a light, when I crawled in, he let out an outward breath of comfort, or relief. I then kissed him lightly on the lips and he fell back to sleep.

I woke up at 5:30am, kissed Chris and slipped out of the bed. I noticed that his skin was very clammy so I gently pulled down the blankets to give him some air. I then went out in the hall to call my mom.

"Merry Christmas, Mom. I know it's early, but I know how early you get up to get things ready on Christmas morning. Could you do me a really big favor? Chris's presents are hidden under my bed, can you bring them to the hospital so when he wakes up, it will feel like Christmas to him?"

"Honey, you are a thoughtful young lady. I would be happy to. If he cannot be home for Christmas, we will bring it to him. I'll be there in about fifteen minutes; I'll meet you in the lobby."

"You are the best, I love you."

"I love you too, honey. See you in a bit."

My mother always knows how eager I am to do certain things and when it comes to Chris, she knows I want him to be happy and healthy. Mom was in the lobby waiting when I got off the elevator, wishing everyone a Merry Christmas.

"Here you go, sweetie. How's he doing?"

"Thanks. He's doing okay I guess. He slept through the night so that was good."

"He needs the rest and he's lucky to have you with him. It's nice that his dad got permission for you to stay."

"Yes it was. Thank you again mom, I'll call you later when I need a ride."

"Okay, honey. Give him a hug for me."

When I got back up to Chris's room, it was swarming with nurses and doctors. I dropped the bag of presents and started crying. From what I gathered, he had a seizure while I was gone. I have to call Cara. I was scared and didn't know what was going on, I called Cara as fast as I could. As I was calling, one of the nurses asked me to wait in the hall and nudged me out and closed the door behind me.

The phone rang several times before it got picked up. "Cara, you have to get to the hospital quick."

"Amanda, honey, calm down, it's Spencer. We're on our way, they've already called us."

"Oh my god, Spencer I'm sorry, I just panicked. He was fine ten minutes ago."

"Amanda, this is not an unusual occurrence when someone has a fever. Try to relax, we'll be there in a few minutes. He's in good hands."

I started crying hysterically. I walked over and sat down, I sat there in complete silence just waiting, waiting for someone to come tell me that he was going to be okay. About 5 minutes later the elevator doors opened and I saw Spencer and Cara rush out. Spencer was still in his scrubs since he'd just gotten home from an emergency surgery and Cara was in her pj's. Spencer rushed right over to the nurse's station and Cara to me. I stood right up. I hugged Cara as tight as I could.

"What's going on?" I asked her. "No one said anything, he was okay all night. I was lying with him and he was asleep. I left for ten minutes and came back to a room full of doctors and nurses."

"Amanda, breathe. It's okay. He's okay. He's going to be okay. Karen and Andrew are watching over him."

I broke down; I didn't know what was going on but I had a bad feeling about it.

As Cara left to talk with Spencer, I sat there with my head on my knees crying. I felt like I just needed to get away from all of this. I lifted my head and saw Spencer and Cara walking toward me. I tried to stand up, but I immediately and fell down to my knees as quick as I stood up.

Spencer came running over and knelt down . "Amanda, are you okay?" He put his hand on my chin and lifted my face up to look at his.

"I'm a mess, I'm sorry. I think I just stood up to quick. Plus I haven't eaten since our family dinner last night."

"It's okay. I thought that's what happened. Here's what happened with Chris. I spoke with the doctor and it seems that the medication that they gave him isn't working. The high fever caused his seizure. They are starting him on a new and stronger one. He should be able to go home in a day or two."

"I left to meet my mom downstairs because I wanted to give Chris his Christmas presents as soon as he woke up. I had no idea this would happen. I just want him to be okay." I stood there wiping my eyes dry while feeling like I was in a dream. Spencer was trying to explain everything to me.

"Seizures take a lot from your body. So why don't we all go home, take a shower, eat, and maybe rest up and come back in a little while?"

Spencer and Cara drove me home. "Amanda, you're his angel," Cara told me. "He's going to be okay. Now eat and get some rest, and we'll see you later." We then wished each other a Merry Christmas, although it didn't feel that merry.

Back in my house, I had a bad feeling in the pit of my stomach and it wouldn't go away. My mom was in the kitchen baking. I sat at the counter watching her, but not really seeing what she was doing. My mind filled with worry.

"Chris had a seizure. I'm so scared; something doesn't feel right to me."

"Honey, seizures, unfortunately are quite common when someone is sick like Chris. It doesn't mean that anything is more wrong with him."

"Everyone keeps telling me that he'll be okay. I don't know mom, something is telling me it won't."

"Amanda, you are exhausted. I think what you should do is go take a shower and lie down. Once you get s bit of sleep, you'll be able to think clearer. Chris needs you to be strong."

"Maybe you're right. Let's keep praying he gets better soon."

"We will honey, now go and get some rest."

As I waited for the water to warm up, all I could think about was that Chris was all alone at the hospital. I didn't want him to be alone. I had to take a quick shower and get back to him.

On my way back to the hospital I headed to 7/11, the only store open on Christmas, to get Chris some of his favorite ice cream and a magazine. When I got back in the car the radio was playing our song and I lost it. Sitting there, trying to compose myself, I jumped at the sound of a tap on the window. It was Ann!

"What are you doing here? I'm so glad to see you." I jumped out of the car.

"I went over to your house to surprise you with my mom's coffee cake and your mom told me what has been going on. I am so sorry about all of this. You should've called me."

"I'm sorry. I've been busy trying to make sure Chris is okay. I can't even think straight. I'm scared, Ann."

She gave me a big hug and squeezed me tight. "I'm here now, so no worries. Let's head on up and see him. I am sure he will love the cake, too."

Ann and I walked into the hospital holding hands. She made me feel better, but that nagging feeling was still in my gut.

"How long will he be here?" she asked me.

"Spencer told me he thought one more day, but my gut tells me it will be a while."

"Well, let's hope his father is right, he's a doctor after all. Think positive Amanda."

"I'm trying."

When the elevator door opened, I saw Spencer, Cara, and a guy I recognized from pictures as Chris's brother, Ryan, standing by the windows talking. They spotted me and smiled. I walked over to them hoping they had some good news.

Ryan reached out his hand. "You must be Amanda. You are just as beautiful as Chris described, if not more. I'm Ryan."

I think I may have blushed a little at his cuteness. He was very handsome. I could definitely see some resemblance, though Ryan is the spitting image of Spencer and Cara. If you didn't know that Chris and Ryan were not biological brothers, you would never know.

"Hi Ryan, nice to meet you."

Ann cleared her throat. I must have forgotten she was with me. I introduced her to Ryan and his parents as well.

"How is Chris doing?" I asked, trying to sound upbeat even though I was afraid what the answer might be.

"He is doing well; I told he was going to be fine. His fever's come down since he started the new medication, and he is getting washed up and changed. We can go in when the nurses come out."

We took a seat while we waited and talked about Christmas until a nurse signaled it was okay for us to go in. We all walked over to his room. They all went ahead of me and said their hellos and gave hugs. Chris watched me from the doorway. Even though he was sick, he was still so very handsome. I walked over to him to kiss his forehead.

Pulling me down on the bed and kissed me hard while giving me a big hug. "Oh, angel, how I've missed you.Where have you been the last few days?"

Feeling confused and the feeling in gut jumped back in. "I was with you last night. I slept here with you."

He looked confused. "Wait, you did? Wasn't that a couple days ago?"

Thankfully Spencer jumped in and started asking questions. "Son, do you know what day it is today?"

He thought about it for a minute then said doubtingly, "Yes it's Christmas Day?"

We both looked at him and said, "Yes it is."

"I'm sorry I must be mixed up, I am kind of tired, well Merry Christmas everyone. I love you all!"

I then felt it again, the feeling that something was very wrong. Trying so hard to erase the feeling, I asked him, "Did you get my Christmas presents?"

He looked very excited. "The nurse told me she found that bag over there on the floor. Is that it?"

I got up and went and picked up the bag, brought it over to him with a huge smile. "Yes, my little gorilla, these are for you.

"Do you want me to open it now or wait till we go home for dinner?"

Cara looked concerned and went over to Chris's side. "Christopher, honey, we aren't going home today. We already talked about this. Remember?"

I looked from Spencer to Cara, we all were feeling the same bit of concern at the moment. Maybe opening the presents will help him feel better. "Are you going to open your presents, Chris?"

"Open the big one first and the small ones after."

He was like an excited five-year-old. "You got me an iPod, Amanda?"

"I sure did. I even downloaded some music on it."

As he was trying to put the plug in the headphone jack he said, "Angel, this is so nice. I love it. It's a perfect gift for me."

I gave him a kiss. "Chris, can you wait to open the others I have to go to the bathroom."

His mom said, "Chris, I have a present for you, too."

I walked out of his room and saw Spencer talking to one of the nurses. I walked over and leaned on the counter putting my elbows on the counter and chin in my hand. I waited patiently for them to finish.

Spencer turned to me. "I know, something seems off here. It could just be a side effect from the seizure, but I asked the nurse to page the doctor for me."

"I know that you're a doctor and I'm just a crazy in love teenager, but I do think there's something very wrong here. I can feel it. I keep getting these weird feelings that something is really wrong." I started crying because I was scared that what I was feeling was right. What if something is terribly wrong here? I shook it off. I took a deep breath.

"I'm sorry, I shouldn't cry. I know that I have to be strong here and be positive. Things will be okay."

Spencer pulled me into a hug. "It will be. My wife told me you had a talk last night. She said she told you all that happened when Chris was a baby. So as you know, Chris is very strong and he has two angels looking over him. He will be okay."

"Thank you."

I hugged him back. I grabbed a tissue wiped my eyes and walked back into Chris's room.

Chris was talking with his mom about Christmas traditions and family. Ann came over to me and said she was going home. She gave me a kiss and Chris a hug and left.

Chris's dad came back with the doctor several minutes later. He asked Chris a bunch of questions and told him they were going to run some more tests that he wanted to make sure the virus was going away. He was thinking that the medication was not strong enough for the virus he had. At that very moment, a nurse walked in and said she was going to take some more blood. I started to feel some relief thinking maybe it was just that the virus was hitting his body hard and the meds weren't working right.

As the nurse took his blood, I could hear the others talking in the hall over my shoulder. I heard a familiar voice. It was Mark, talking to a nurse. When he spotted me, he smiled and started walking toward the door. I got up and gave him a kiss on the cheek. He was holding a gift basket of goodies in his arms. I thanked him for being there for Chris and for me as usual. I loved that he was always there for me just like Ann was.

Mark and Ann have always been my rocks. Both of them have been there for me anytime I needed a friend. Today proved that they were here for Chris too.

"Look Chris, Mark brought you some goodies."

Mark went over to Chris while I took the basket over to the shelf in the corner of the room. They were happily talking about sports while I just stood in the corner.

Now that Chris seemed stable, she was going back to the house to finish making Christmas Lunch so she could bring Chris his favorites when she came back. She told me to call her if I needed anything. I told her I would. They both gave Chris a kiss and they left. Then his brother said he was going to run an errand and he too would be back in a bit. Then he left too. I thought maybe I should call my dad and let him know I might not be joining them for Christmas. I really wanted to stay by Chris's side.

I dug my phone out of my pocketbook when I saw that he had already called me. He left a message but I figured I would call and talk with him. I was listening to the phone ring while watching the boys laugh at something. It really was nice to see them laughing even when it's in these circumstances. I loved that they got along; it made me happy knowing that Chris wasn't jealous of mine and Mark's friendship.

As I was sitting there watching the two guys I loved, talk and laugh I hadn't even realized my Dad had answered the phone.

"Oh, I'm sorry Dad, what's up?"

He said laughing, "I thought maybe you pocket dialed me."

I wondered how long I let him hang there while he was saying my name and trying to get my attention.

"No, Dad, sorry. I was kind of spaced out while I was waiting for you to answer."

"No apologies, Amanda. Really it's okay. I called because I wanted to let you know that your mom called me and told me what was going on. Are you okay?"

As I sat there and thought about how much my life had changed, I couldn't help but smile. Both my mom and dad were happy, and we all had a strong relationship now. I had friends who cared about me and a boyfriend who loved me.

"Yeah...Dad, thank you. I'm okay. I'm at the hospital with Chris and Mark now. The doctors are running more blood tests. They think that it's just that the meds aren't strong enough for this virus he has. He'll probably be here for another day or two depending on the meds."

As soon as I got those words out of my mouth my whole body was consumed with worry.

"Well, we'll all be here at your Grammies' if you want to stop by. Aunt Marie said she is thinking of you and praying for Chris. I'll let you get back to him. I hope you can stop by for at least a little while honey. But I love you and understand if you don't get to."

"Okay, Dad, thank you. I'll do my best to make it over. In the meantime, give everyone a kiss for me. I love you too, Dad."

I was thirsty so I decided to take a walk to the cafeteria to get something to drink. I took the stairs to burn some energy.At the cafeteria, I grabbed a few different things I knew Chris liked as well. As I was walking back, I spotted someone I recognized in the ER waiting area. My mouth fell open and I dropped all the stuff I was holding on the floor. I stood there feeling like I could fall to the floor at any moment myself.

I felt a hand on my shoulder and someone was talking to me, asking me if I was okay. I turned to find an older man talking to me. I stutteringly told him I was fine. He bent down helping to pick up the stuff that I had dropped on the floor when I realized that the guy that I saw had now spotted me too. I bent down quickly, thanking the man for helping me. As I finished gathering my stuff, I started to stand.

I went to turn and walk the other way when I heard my name called. I stopped dead in my tracks; I stood there not knowing if I could even move another step. I had to get the hell out of here. I started walking faster to the stairs, as I knew I couldn't get far having to wait for the elevators. As I reached for the door, I heard my name again. My blood started to boil and I was heating very fast with anxiousness and fury that was consuming me. I pushed the door open and started up the stairs taking two at a time.

I kept hearing him call my name and I yelled out, "Leave me the hell alone." I was going as fast as I could up the stairs when I felt a hand grab my arm. I stopped dead in my tracks yet again. I felt his hand squeeze my arm while he said my name, again. I let out the breath I was holding before I passed out from lack of oxygen. That's all I needed was to pass out and fall down three flights of stairs.

"Brad, let go of me right now before I punch you in the face and push you down the stairs."

My heart was practically pounding through my chest. If our bodies didn't have a rib cage to protect our hearts, mine for sure would have ripped through my skin. It was pounding so hard. My face was hot and I was fuming. How dare he even think about talking to me, let alone touch me? All of a sudden, I thought I might throw up.

"I'm sorry, Amanda. I saw you and needed to talk to you."

I took a deep breath to try to keep the bile from coming up.

"I told you if you ever saw me again to keep on your way and act like you didn't know me."

"Believe me when I say, I meant every fucking word. You raped me and I hate you more than you could ever imagine."

I turned in lightning speed, I darted up the stairs. I couldn't get away from him fast enough. I think he was in shock because he stood there not saying a word, and he didn't follow me.

I got up to the door and opened it with force. I stood on the other side of the door trying to compose myself. When the door behind me slammed shut, I jumped slightly. I stood there for another moment just breathing. I then started toward Chris's room. I got about a little more than half way there, when I heard my name called yet again.

I stopped, not knowing if I should keep on to Chris's room, I wouldn't want him to follow me there. I turned and said loudly, "Brad I have nothing to say to you. Nor do I wish to hear anything you have to say. Being as all that comes out of your mouth are lies anyway. Leave me alone and please stop following me."

I felt a hand on my shoulder when I heard Mark say, "Brad what are you doing here?"

"I am down in the ER with Mom waiting on Dad. They think he had a small heart attack."

"Brad, I'm sorry, I had no idea. How's he doing?"

"We don't know yet, they haven't let us back to see him"

I turned to Mark. "Mark I am sorry. He didn't say anything to me about your uncle, but could you just get him out of here, please, before I have a heart attack of my own."

Brad started saying my name as Mark was walking toward him. I paused just before Chris's door as I watched them.

"Brad, why don't you go wait with your mom, I'm sure she's wondering where you went to."

"Mark, I have something I need to say to Amanda."

"Brad, listen to me. Now is not the time. Your dad is sick and he needs you focusing on him, not the past. Come on I will go wait with you."

I looked at him with all sincerity and said, "Brad, I'm sorry about your Dad. I hope he is okay but please, I have nothing to say to you. Just please leave me alone."

I continued into Chris's room, I put a smile on my face and said, "Hey I got some snacks for us." Chris looked at what I had in my arms and smiled.

He started talking when Brad abruptly interrupted us. He rushed into Chris's room; he didn't make it all the way in. Mark was holding him back.

"Brad, buddy, I know you're upset about your dad and you obviously need to vent something but this is not the time or place to do that. You need to leave now and go be with your mother. I'll come with you."

"Mark get him the hell out of here before I call security myself. Brad I told you that I have nothing to say to you."

I felt Chris's hand on mine. "Amanda, who is that? What is going on?"

"Sorry Chris to upset you with this nonsense, nothing, and he is nobody."

I turned back and said with a yell, "I said get the fuck out now."

Storming past them while Mark had his hands wound tight around Brads arms; I quickly passed them to get to the nurse's station. All the while, Mark and Brad were bickering back and forth. I politely and calmly asked the nurse to call security and have this guy escorted back down to the ER. She was picking up the phone when Brad started talking to me.

"Amanda...will you just talk to me for a minute, please. I need to tell you that I am sorry that I hurt you, I'm sorry. I did love you and I didn't want to hurt you. I have lived with it for the last three years what I did to you."

I could feel my face getting red. I couldn't believe he was doing this. Then I saw the guards coming out of the corner of my eye and I had relief. I cannot talk to him about this now or ever, for that matter. I just wanted him gone. Mark was trying to push him toward the waiting area and elevators. Now that Mark and Brad were not blocking the door, I could see Chris. He was sitting up and was turned toward the door in his bed. He had a look of sadness and extreme curiosity on his face. He could see me. With the tears now streaming full on and down my face. I just stood there. I was staring at Chris with that look on his face and he was staring at me knowing me all too well. He knew that something happened to me that really hurt me. Then I knew at that moment I could not get out of this. I was going to have to tell him. I fell to my knees; I put my head down and my hands on my face. I had lost it. I was trying so hard to have this not affect me. I need to be strong. I need to stay positive and happy for Chris.

Now here I was a crying mess on the floor of the hospital as he watched me helplessly. I couldn't believe this was all happening right now. I could hear commotion going on with Brad. Then I felt hands on my arms, it was Mark.

"Amanda, it's okay. He's gone now. Let's try and calm down, for Chris's sake."

He was trying to help me up. I felt like a fool. I was a mess and I couldn't stop the tears from falling. I could hear Chris calling my name. He sounded so sad.

Mark said to me in a whisper, "Amanda you haven't told him yet? You should tell him, he has a right to know. You have nothing to be ashamed about. You know what happened to you was not your fault. Chris loves you and you love him. You should tell him what happened to you. Let him understand your past. I know you and you are worried that he will look at you differently. That he will not love you the same once he finds out. But you need to know that it's not going to happen. I think he will be supportive. He will understand. Amanda, you need to get up and go talk to him, he's calling you. Don't leave him wondering."

I realized he was right; I did need to tell Chris. Hell after this show now I had no choice. I let

Mark help me up; he helped back to the room. I walked in with my head down.

"Honey, are you okay? What's wrong?"

"Chris, I think Amanda needs to tell you some things. Are you feeling well enough to talk?"

He spoke clearing his throat and said, "Of course I am. Amanda sit with me let's talk."

Mark spoke while grabbing his stuff and said, "Well I am gonna go downstairs and check on my uncle and make sure that Brad stays down there. I will see you two love birds later." He leaned over, kissed my head, and whispered, "It all will be okay."

"Thank you Mark. I will talk to you later and I hope your uncle is okay." He left as I sat on Chris's bed unsure of exactly where to start so I just did the best I could. "Chris first, I want to apologize for all that, I feel like a fool."

He took my face in his hands. "Amanda, you don't need to apologize. It's obvious that Brad guy hurt you in some way and you don't have to talk about it if you don't want to. I will understand. You can take your time and tell me when your ready. I just don't want to see you hurting or upset; it breaks my heart, honestly." He kissed me on the forehead and gave me an assuring smile.

I loved that he was so caring. "No it's okay," I said. "I don't need to take time. But I do want to make sure you feel well enough to talk about this because I don't want to upset you."

"I am fine to talk. Come on, I am fine. It's just a little virus that's all. Now get talking. Tell me all about what that scumbag did to you."

I chucked at the way he said that. Even in serious times, he makes me laugh. "Okay, well as I had told you before there are things I didn't really talk about, for a long time my past was one of them." I paused for a moment trying to gather myself, and then I continued, "So what I never told you was that I had a very crappy childhood. My Mom and Dad were two very different people when I was younger. My Mom had been in many very abusive relationships, which unfortunately, I had witnesses more than I should have. My Mom was poor and struggled a lot. She got into drugs bad for a while but she is good now and has been for a long time now, about 7 years. I took a deep breath and he grabbed my hand holding it firmly. Jim actually is the first guy that has never hit her out of all her many boyfriends, like all eight of them. We moved probably ten times since I was a baby. My Dad and I spent as much time together as we could. All of my family never knew about what was going on at my home. I never told anyone until recently. My Mom always hiding it, one guy beat her so bad and she told people she was in a car accident, and then hid her car for a week pretending it was in the shop getting fixed. Anyway, I started hanging around with Kelly a lot when I was fourteen. Do you remember Kelly Hart? He shrugged his shoulders and made a face indicating kind of. Well, I started hanging with her and we partied a lot. We hung with older guys too. That is when I met Brad. He's actually Marks cousin if you hadn't gathered that they are related." Shifting in the bed and adjusting myself to get comfortable.

Anyway, we dated for a few months. He was a huge mistake; I should have never even dated him. An older guy, I don't know what I was thinking. Honestly, I wasn't really thinking at all, besides I liked getting attention from a cute guy, I was too young and needless to say, he was too advanced for me. It actually makes me sick just thinking about it.

Chris then piped in and said laughing, "Well don't throw up on me, please. I hate puke." I smirked at him and said I wouldn't. It's nice he is trying to lighten this up a bit.

I continued, "So after dating for a bit, we had conversations about me not being ready and all that. He agreed to take things slow. Until one day, he came to my house and things got heated between us as we made out. He ended up telling me that he loved me that day. Before I knew it, he was on top of me and I froze. Completely froze. I was scared and I knew what was about to happen, then I came to and said No. I told him that I didn't want to." Feeling hesitant to continue I'm wondering what he's thinking.

From the moment, I had said he was on top of me I felt Chris tense up. I knew he was trying to prepare himself. I think he knew what I was going to say. I could feel him start to shake when I started talking again. "But needless to say he did it anyway."

Chris gasped when I said it and his grip on my hand grew tighter. I put my head down and let the tears I was holding back fall. I knew that I wasn't going to be able to keep them back anyway. When it came to this, it really killed me to have to admit that I was raped. I was young and not ready and here I was admitting to Chris who has shown he really loves me. He has shown me patience and has never once pressured me into more than I was ready for and here I was telling him that another guy tainted me.

He then found the words he was holding back and said loudly, "That fucker raped you?"

I suddenly heard a gasp coming from the doorway. I immediately looked up to see his parents. I then felt even more red flush my cheeks.

I thought I was going to die. My day couldn't get any worse. I put my head down.

"Mom, Dad, how long have you been standing there?"

His dad spoke up, probably because his Mom was still in shock from what she had just overheard. He said, "Sorry Chris. We were only here a minute."

"We were having a private conversation." Chris seemed agitated that they had overheard.

His mom rushed over to me. "Oh my Amanda, is this true? Are you hurt? Are you okay?"

"Mom, she is okay. She was just telling me something that was obviously private."

Cara choked back a sob. "I'm sorry that we overheard your private conversation, and Amanda I am so very sorry that this has happened to you. But can I ask why you are talking about this now?"

I gasped to myself and froze thinking, she is right I should have waited. I started to get up to leave when Chris strongly pulled me back to him.

He held me tight and said, "Apparently the guy that did it is downstairs in the ER with his dad. He spotted Amanda when she went down to get us a snack. Then he proceeded to follow her back up here and started making a scene until security came and took him back down."

At that moment, I could only imagine the look on his parents faces. I was so embarrassed; I knew they were all looking at me. I could feel there stares. I couldn't help but wonder if they were judging me? What did they think of me now? Then Chris spoke again asking his parents to leave for a few minutes. Maybe go grab some coffee at the Starbucks that was downstairs.

As I sat there quiet just being held by Chris, I felt at ease. Telling Chris my secret made me feel a little better. I lay in his arms quietly. He was relaxing and his breath was starting to steady. I wondered how long we would go before talking.

"I am not a fighter but he better pray that I never run into him. I am so angry at what he did to you. What a pathetic excuse for a man."

I loved that he would want to defend me but the last thing I would want would be for them to fight. "Chris if you ever see him, don't engage. Don't say anything to him. He is not worth it. I promise you it is something that I have accepted and moved on from. You just have to understand that it was just hard for me to come clean and tell you. I didn't want you to have a bad image of me. I didn't want your feelings for me to change. It did take a long time for me to accept that it wasn't my fault. But I don't want to linger on what happened. I am happy I told you. I am sorry that it took so long. But from this point on, can we please leave it here. Can we not talk about it anymore?"

He looked down at me and smiled his sweet smile. "Yes anything for you my love." I smiled back at him then moved in for a kiss.

His kisses warmed me and made me feel so happy. I had a thought to maybe take a nap with him but I leaned over him to grab the iPod I bought him, and he laughed as my breasts brushed his arm.

I laughed and pulled back and said, "Let's take a nap cowboy and listen to some music." We both put an ear bud in our ear and dozed off in peace.

We woke a while later to her the nurse talking to his parents. When I opened my eyes, they were sitting in the chairs across from the bed reading the paper.

When they realized that we were awake Cara said, "Hey sleepy heads. We came in to you two sound asleep and we didn't want to wake you. Ryan stopped by as well and said he will see you tomorrow. But you two lovebirds must be hungry would you like to eat? I cooked us all a nice early dinner. I have it downstairs in the cafeteria. They said they would heat it up when we were ready." We both shook our heads eagerly indicating that we were starved. She called down and told the kitchen we were ready to eat. I loved that we had the hook up here, as hospitals did tend to have bad food.

As we waited for our food to arrive, his parents wanted us to open our presents. His mom walked over and handed us the gifts they had gotten us.

We both looked at each other and said, "Go" just like we were kids. His parents laughed. I think they thought it was cute. But after the day we both had already, we needed some excitement. We tore through the paper and got to the surprises inside. I couldn't believe it; they got me a digital camera.

"Wow, this is amazing, thank you so much." I looked over to see what Chris got and they got him the same one. We both looked at one another and smiled. I was just happy I could now capture our times together. Knowing him, he was happy because now he could continue to take random pictures of me when I wasn't looking. We both thanked his parents again. They told us that they just wanted to give us something that we could keep forever. What better than pictures to capture our memories.

I loved that they were so thoughtful. They then told us that they were all charged and ready to go. We could use them to capture our first Christmas. His Mom wasn't even done saying that and Chris already had the box open. I loved that he was so eager. He turned the camera on and handed it to his mom.

"Mom, will you please take the first picture of me and my angel." He turned to look at me and my heart melted yet again. We touched our foreheads together, smiling at one another, taking in a moment of peace and happiness when his mom snapped the first picture.

She said, "I love it. You two are so in love and so happy."

He leaned in and gave me a kiss saying, "Me too" when she snapped another picture. We both broke apart from the kiss and started laughing. We weren't expecting that picture.

"Me too," I said. "I love him and I am so happy."

Then there was a knock at the door. Our food arrived. It was all arranged on a small cart and it had everything we needed. Cara then snapped another picture of the food on the cart. Chris looked like he was ready to drool. I heard his stomach growl at that very moment.

"Well I guess I am hungrier than I thought." We started laughing again when Cara snapped another. She was going picture crazy with the new camera.

We ate our meal and it was wonderful. I was so full, I couldn't eat one more bite. Chris and I lay back in his bed. As we both looked at each other with a look of complete satisfaction. Then this time it was Spencer that snapped a picture of us.

"I love it, the way you two look at each other. I couldn't help myself."

All of a sudden, Chris said, "Honey, you haven't opened my present yet."

"No I didn't. Would you like me too now?" He shook his head yes, as he sipped on a glass of water. Cara then brought over a gift. It was a little box. The size of a jewelry box. "Come on open it."

I started unwrapping his gift slowly. When I took the paper off tit revealed a black velvet box. I opened the box to find a very beautiful necklace. It was silver with diamonds, in the shape of a G clef. It was beautiful. "Oh Chris, I love it."

I gave him a great big hug and kiss on the cheek. All the while, his parents took pictures. He put the necklace on for me then he gave me another kiss.

A short while later his parents decided to call it a night and go home. Leaving us to have some time alone. We lay in his bed and cuddled. We listened to his iPod, after a few songs is when he finally started to sing. I knew it was coming and I loved every second of it. There were times when I wanted to sing along with him but I just enjoyed his voice so much. I will wait and just enjoy him and the music.

As we laid our legs intertwined together, he lightly rubbing his fingers in random patterns on my arm. I did the same on his stomach. I think we really both enjoyed the selection of music he had on it. It really amazes me how much we had in common. I know that I love music but there was not one song that I didn't like.

After many songs played, I took the ear bud out and told him that I was gonna go home soon, and that he probably would get better rest if we both weren't squeezed into this twin size bed anyway.

He got a sad puppy dogface and told me, "No, I don't want you to go; I sleep so much better when you are with me. I like being close to you. Will you please stay with me? My dad already talked to the nurses. Please?"

I looked at him with a very happy smile and confessed, "There is nothing that I would love more than to stay with you. I also sleep better when I am with you. Even if it is squashed into this little bed." I said as I squeezed onto the bed with him.

He said, "Thank you, this means a lot to me you know." With a big smile, he handed me my ear bud back. I put it into my ear just as a new song was about to start.

As the first notes, started playing when I realized that it was one of the songs I selected to add onto his list. I looked up at him, waiting for him to realize it was a new one. I love this song; it fits us well especially in this moment. Then he sang the next line while looking into my eyes. "Looking in your eyes, seeing all I need, everything you are is everything to me." I stretched up and gave him a nice and tender kiss. It made warmth spread through my body. It made me ache inside to be with him again. I slowly broke away from him knowing I wanted to sing the next verse to him.

"And every prayer has been answered and every dream I've had's come true." Now he bent down and gives me a kiss that lit me on fire. This kiss made it really hard to keep it together. I thought, Oh boy this is going to be a long night. Especially if we keep singing and kissing each other like this. So I said, "We might have to pretend this is a hotel room and stick a 'Do not disturb' sign on the door."

He laughed and said, "Or college and just put a sock on it."

A moment later, he realized he needed to go to the bathroom. So he got up and walked with his IV to the bathroom. As he walked, I could not contain myself as his Jonny was open in the back and I could see his perfect ass peeking out at me. I had some kind of dirty thoughts for when he gets back to bed. I started to laugh and made a comment when there was a knock on the door. "Honey quick someone might see your ass." I waited till he was in the bathroom. "Come on in!"

It was the night nurse. As she came into the room "Hi Amanda I just need to get Chris' temperature, blood pressure, and check his IV."

"He just went to the bathroom." I was happy that it was the same nurse from last night because she was very nice for letting me stay. I figured I mention that I was staying again tonight. "Hey Elaine! Did Dr. Jenkins already tell you I might stay?"

She smiled at me and said, "Sure sweetie yes he did that is fine. I will just check him and then I will let you two get some rest."

I think it helps that our parents work here in the hospital. Thinking of it, I figured I should call my poor mother who really hasn't seen much of me today. I leaned over, grabbed my bag, and pulled out my phone. I called my mom and luckily, I didn't wake her up. "Hey mom, I just wanted to let you know that I am going to spend the night at the hospital again with Chris. He doesn't want to stay alone and I just can't seem to leave him."

"Okay, I figured that. But tomorrow I will see you right?"

"Most definitely, Mom. I love you."

"I love you too, honey. Goodnight."

Just as I hung up, Chris walked out of the bathroom. I figured I would go while she is checking him out. I don't want to be in the way. I grabbed my bag and headed for the bathroom again.

I came out of the bathroom after freshening up, Chris was lying in the bed, and the nurse had gone. He had that sexy smile on his face. I got excited, ran over, and hopped into bed. He turned into me and said, "Have I told you today that I love you?"

I smiled and said, "Umm let me think yes, but can you tell me again?"

He had the biggest grin on his face and said, "Amanda my angel, I love you, I am so much in love with you it hurts. I am very thankful for you and happy that you are here with me. Thank you for spending the night." All I could do was just kiss him. He has this way about him that every time he says things to me he just warms me up.

I pulled away from the kiss and said, "Well Christopher, I love you too and I am so very thankful that we have found one another. I am also am very happy to be here with you and did I ever tell you that every single time you say my name, kiss me, touch me, or tell me you love me; you warm me and make my heart melt. I know that this all may sound corny but it's true. You have this way of completely making me feel your love for me every time we are together and I just feel like I am on cloud nine. I truly never thought I would be this happy."

He wrapped his arms around me and held me tight. As we lay together, just holding each other I felt the feeling that we will be together forever. He is the man of my dreams, my soul mate, and one day I will marry him. Even though I am young I am sure of this. No doubt in my mind about it.

I pulled back from him a little, he was holding me so tight, almost like if he let up at all I, would disappear. I looked into his baby blue eyes seeing all I needed in them. I then put my lips on his and we instantly picked up where we left off before the bathroom break. The passion and heat flooded back like someone just flipped a switch. My hand was in his messy bed head, the other trapped under me. One of his hands was wrapped in my hair, holding my head so I wouldn't pull away again. While his other hand was on the small of my back pressing on it as if to keep me close.

Our legs were wrapped together and I could feel the desire he had for me pressing on my belly. At this very moment, I know I needed him; I needed him to be closer to me, to be inside me. We needed to be as one. He had me so consumed by his love that this need felt so strong I thought I would die if I didn't have him. I had no cares that we were in the hospital. And I don't think at that moment he did either. We just desperately needed each other.

I wiggled my arm out from under me to find his skin. I needed to touch him, and I wanted to feel his desire for me. My hand naturally, with no struggles, found his hardness. I began to move my hand, lightly stroking him and I smiled into the kiss just as he did. As he moved the hand, he had on my back. He slid it down into my pants and gently squeezed my ass, pulling me into him. I knew at that moment that I was not going to be able to hold off for long.

I told him, "Chris I need you so bad, I can't stand it.

He said into the kiss, "I need you too. It feels like it has been too long since I've been inside of you."

I started slowly moving my mouth down his chin, I moved to his neck nibbling on his ear a little then I kept going, I stopped when I got down to his hardness. I kissed the head of his cock, which was already gleaming with his moisture. I licked him then wrapped my hot mouth over him, working my way all the way down. When I got to the bottom and his hair tickled my nose. I slowly pulled my head back up. He let out a low growl from his throat. I licked over his length a few times. He put his hands on my head pulling me back up to him. I put my mouth over his and worked my tongue into his mouth. He was reaching down trying to pull off my pants, when I quickly hopped off the bed and stepped out of my pants. I had on a red-laced thong I bought special for Christmas; I slowly pulled them down, stepping out of them the whole time, keeping my eyes on him. I could see the amount of desire he had in his eyes. It burned so hot that it made his eyes look a deeper blue.

I climbed back into the bed straddling him and bent down to find his tender lips; I kissed him deeply with all that I had, and said, "Chris I love you so much, I don't ever want to be apart from you. I feel whole when I am with you. I want you all the time. I feel I am a tad obsessed. I try to contain myself but it is so hard."

I lifted up and gently guided him to me. I placed him at my opening and then slowly sank down on him. Little by little, I let him fill me, expanding slowly to adjust to him; he was so hard inside of me. He was now filling me completely. I sat on top of him and bent down to kiss his lips again, but instead he met me half way. Now he was in the sitting position. I wrapped my arms around him, kissing him passionately and I started to move up and down. I let a moan escape my lips. Having him inside me truly made me feel complete. He fit so perfectly there. As we continued on making love slow and passionate, he quickly flipped me over so that I was on my back under his weight; he adjusted his IV into a good place. Before putting himself back into me he bent down and kissed me while his fingers found my wetness. He worked his finger up and found my sweet spot. He worked his finger in slow circles. As he moved his hand, I could feel the ache building between my legs and in my core. I knew it wouldn't be long before I exploded with ecstasy. Just when it started to build up and I started to feel my inner muscles begin to tighten as I moaned into his ear.

He guided himself back into me. Moving so slow above me, I could start to feel that pressure build again. I moved myself down about an inch so as he moved in and out; he would rub the spot he was just touching. I closed my eyes as they were starting to roll back into my head. The feeling was building up so strong inside that I knew it was coming. I reached up and treaded my fingers thru his hair, pulling him to my mouth, he let out a groan. He put his lips to mine and as soon as his tongue brushed mine, I exploded. Feeling my release that had built up, I could not help or stop the sounds that came from me at that moment. It was as if my body kept going. It didn't stop. As he picked up the pace a little, my legs started to tremble and yet another wave of ecstasy washed over me. I could now feel my whole body start to tremble. As I could tell he was almost ready, his breath was starting to hitch when all the sudden he got harder inside of me. I could feel him filling me. His hotness spread through me as he let go. I shook slightly from what I think was an aftershock of such an intense orgasm. I felt a single tear slip down my cheek.

Whispering he said, "Amanda, I love you. Stay, stay with me forever."

As I looked into his eyes, I could see that what he was saying to me was coming from his heart. Cause his eyes were telling me the same thing. Don't leave me. As he wiped the tears off my cheek, I said, "I love you too Christopher, I will not leave you, ever."

We lay holding each other for a while. When I thought I might fall asleep, I got up and put my pants back on. I would hate someone to walk in and see my ass. I climbed back into bed, putting on the iPod and handing one of the buds to Chris; he smiled at me and said, "That was truly amazing. I love being inside of you, I feel that we are one and I love it, but even just being with you is enough for me." We lay holding each other. Singing low to the music until I surrendered to sleep. While listening to him sing.

Crash and Burn

In the morning, I woke to light music filling my head. Chris was rubbing my back while stopping every so often and drawing patterns with his fingers. I looked up at him and he flashed his handsome smile at me.

"Good morning," I said. Aren't you just a happy sight to wake up to."

"I am aren't I? You are too." He then reached over and put something on the table. I pulled my head up to see what it was. I gasped when I saw it was the camera.

"Chris you better not have taken pictures of me when I was sleeping."

He chuckled and said, "Why what will happen if I did. Besides, you have nothing to worry about anyway. You didn't drool and you are very beautiful when you sleep. Your like sleeping beauty."

I laughed and said, "Yeah right."

He said, "Are you hungry?"

"Yes very."

"Good because I called down to the front desk and ordered us some room service." I looked at him with panic and confusion as I wondered if maybe he was forgetting again. "What? Don't look at me like that."

"Chris, we are in a hospital. They don't have room service."

He laughed. "Honey, I know, I am joking with you. I thought you would get it. Remember last night we you said we should put the do not disturb sign on the door."

Rubbing my forehead. "I can't believe I didn't catch that one."

As I said that there was a light knock at the door, it was the kitchen with our "room service." I was so happy he ordered me pancakes and bacon. Same thing we ate for breakfast the first night I slept over his house. We sat and ate our breakfast and just as we were finishing, Chris's parents and brother showed up.

"Ok now that your family is here I'm gonna go home and shower. I'll come back in a bit." I gave him a kiss " I'll be back shortly. Will you guys be here when I get back?"

Cara responded, "Yeah we should be. I planned on sticking around today." I said bye to everyone but before leaving. I told his parents he was

While I was walking down to my car, I spotted Mark. He was just leaving the hospital too. I yelled to him, as he did not see me. He turned back to see me and he just smirked at me. He looked sad. At that very moment, I realized that his uncle must have not made it. I quickly rushed to catch up to him. Grabbing his arm as he was still walking.

"Mark, stop. Talk to me."

He stopped walking and turned to me. "Well I have nothing to say really. I am just trying to think about how I will go tell my mom that her brother just died."

My heart felt really heavy. "It's okay. I will come with you."

"She is on her way here right now. I called her a little while ago to tell her I was here and what was going on with him. She had a quick meeting at work so I came ahead of her. I just don't get it he was alive a little while ago. He was fine last night and this morning. He was talking to me and everything. All of the sudden had another massive heart attack and died on the spot. That was the most devastating thing I have ever witnessed."

"Oh Mark. I am so sorry for your loss. This is terrible." I leaned in and gave him a long hard consoling hug. "Let's go grab a coffee while we wait for your mom." We walked over to the Starbucks in the lobby and I treated him to a latte. We took a seat near the front door waiting for his mom to arrive.

"I am sure you're busy. Please feel free to leave. I'll be fine."

"No way. I am here for you, no matter what."

I spotted his mom and nudged him to let him know she had arrived. He looked up and stood. I followed him over to the doors. "Mark that face...What's wrong. Oh my god, please tell me he is okay?" My heart sank down to my feet. He handed me his cup then quickly put his arms around his mom.

Squeezing her tightly he said, "No, Mom. I am sorry. He's gone."

I will never forget the look on her face. My heart broke for them. I stayed with them for a little while as we waited there for Mark's aunt to come out. He was going to drive them home.

I wrapped my arms around Mark. "Call me later if you want. I don't care what time it is."

I spotted Brad busting through the doors. He was loudly rambling something when Mark let go to face him.

"I will talk to you later. Hang in there." I told him. I started to walk away but stopped to watch Mark tell Brad that his father had passed away. Brad fell to his knees, hitting the floor with a thud. My heart felt saddened for them. Brad too, even though I despised him. I still felt bad for him. Mark nodded for me to leave. So I blew him a kiss and left.

I felt awful for Mark's family. I called Ann. She picked up after a few rings.

"Ann, oh my, you will never guess what happened. I can't even believe it all myself. I feel like I'm in a bad dream or something." I continued to tell her about all that happened yesterday and today.

"Oh my god, Amanda, that is crazy. So you want to send Mark and his mom a fruit arrangement? I know it doesn't replace there loss but maybe it will make them eat a little."

"That's a great idea. You wanna order it and we can split the bill? Hey so I will call you later and we can make plans to get together."

I hung up from her and went into my house. I quickly showered, changed, and ate a little, then decided to go back to the hospital and see my love.

On my way back to the hospital I listened to the new CD Chris made me. I was singing along like I was a good singer when the song cut out abruptly; my was phone ringing. I hit my Bluetooth button again to accept the call. It was Cara. My heart dropped quickly because I knew she had no need to call me.

Hesitantly I answered. "Hey, Cara whats up?" I said, trying not to be to chipper, but also calm at the same time.

"Amanda, are you on your way back to the hospital?" She sounded like she had been crying. So naturally my gut turned into a giant knot instantly.

"Ahh yeah I'm just about to pull into the parking lot now. Why? Is everything okay?" I asked with even more hesitation. I paused waiting for an answer and all I got was silence so I responded quick so she didn't have to talk. "Yeah Cara I will be there in a couple of minutes."

I pulled into the first spot I could find, and grabbed my bag as I jumped out of my car. My heart was nearly coming out of my throat. I ran thru the front doors and spotted Brad yet again, he was talking to a nurse. He ran over to me and grabbed my arm. I yelled at him. "Let me go. I have nothing else to say to you."

"I just want to talk to you for a minute. It will be quick." I don't even know why he was talking to me. I was very clear with him yesterday.

I yelled at him, "Brad let me go."

"Give me just one damn minute to talk to you and I will."

I moved closer to him and said loudly and sternly in his face with anger, "You need to let me go right now. The man I LOVE is upstairs. He is sick and he needs me. Something is wrong. Now fucking let go." I ripped my arm from his tight grasp and turned away.

As I was rushing to the stairway I heard him "We will talk Amanda."

I ran as fast as I could to the stairs. I think I took them a whole flight at a time. I went so quickly. Something was wrong. Very, very wrong. I burst through the door and ran down the hall. As I approached Chris's room, I slowed myself while putting my hand on the door. I grasped the handle tightly while taking what I think was the deepest breath of my life. Almost as if it was my last...

The End...

I know cliffhangers...Sorry!

Part 2 will be coming soon.

ABOUT THE AUTHOR

Melinda is a new author who came quickly crashing into writing. She started writing after being inspired by many great Authors. Those Authors to name a few being S.C. Stephens, Jasinda Wilder, and Abbey K. Davies. Abbey was the final push that made her want to get the story she's had floating around in her head for a long time out.

She lives in a small New England town with her loving and supportive husband and two young boys. She finds inspiration in other authors, music, her amazing family, friends, and of course her very amusing co-worker. Melinda really enjoys reading, now writing, taking pictures, massages, coffee, chocolate, ice cream, and beer & wine. She loves spending her free time playing with her boys, taking family trips, spending time with loved ones, going on quiet dates with her husband, and crazy fun nights out with her girlfriends.

Acknowledgments

I'd like to thank some people
who helped to make this book come to life...

First all of you who encouraged me to get this book
back up there...THANK YOU!

Cover Designer: Renee Ericson

Editor First Edition: Kristen Baker

Editor Second Edition: Francine Lasala

Betas: Jennifer Short-Benson, Chelsea Camaron,
Carey Heywood, Saoching Moose, Kristen Baker,
Amy Barber McGlone & Annie Gabor

Bloggers: I thank each & every one of you who
helped share my new cover & book.

Especially my girls at: Hooked on Books,
Turn the Page & Book Geeks Unite

Author Friends & Motivators:

Abbey K. Davies, Kendall Grey, Jasinda Wilder,
Jade C. Jamison, Renee Ericson, Jennifer
LaRocca, Kasey Millstead, and S.C. Stephens
(even though she don't know it)

To all my friends & family for your support and for listening to me vent especially you poor girls...

LeeAnne, Carrie, Angela, Lynne, Monica, Jill, Annie, Terri

&

My Husband for all your patience, support and understanding. For being an amazing Dad. And I cannot forget to thank you for buying me a new mac & desk so I could write stress free. I love you!

Made in the USA
Charleston, SC
30 July 2013